Sam has been living in the forest since his parents were killed and his brother taken because of what they were—unicorn shifters. He hasn't approached the wolf pack living nearby because he doesn't know if he can trust them, but when he meets a wolf at the stream and realizes they're mates, he knows he will have to get over that distrust.

Frederic didn't expect to meet his mate in the forest where the pack lives, and he certainly didn't expect his mate to be a unicorn shifter. Sam is, though, and he comes with complications and problems—and Frederic is willing to take them all on.

Sam is wary and doesn't know how to trust, but he hopes having the pack's help means he can finally look for his brother. He doesn't know where to start, though, so using himself as bait for the men who killed his parents sounds like a good idea.

Until it doesn't.

For the Love of a Unicorn

ISBN: 978-1-4874-2413-8
Cover art by Angela Waters

Published by eXtasy Books Inc or
Devine Destinies, an imprint of eXtasy Books Inc

Look for us online at:
www.eXtasybooks.com or www.devinedestinies.com

For the Love of a Unicorn
Legendary Shifters Book 1

By

Catherine Lievens

Chapter One

Sam trotted toward the stream. His mouth was dry, and he wanted to take a bath, but the stream wasn't deep enough for that. He'd have to settle for getting his hooves and mouth wet he supposed, maybe his belly. He was also hungry, though, so he couldn't stay long. He'd noticed some nice grass in a clearing just off the stream. If he was lucky, he'd leave this place with his belly full and cleaner than he'd been in a while.

He resisted the urge to jump into the stream, but he *did* walk into it. The water felt good against the skin above his hooves. He dipped his nose into the water, ignoring his reflection, and wiggled it. He huffed, creating bubbles, and finally drank.

Where had this stream been in the past years? He couldn't remember it, yet he knew most of the forest he'd been roaming. It would be hard not to. It had to have been at least a year since he'd lost his family.

A pang of pain made him close his eyes. He shouldn't think about that. It wouldn't help. If anything, it would make things worse for him. It always did, because then he started thinking bad thoughts, like that maybe he should have died with his parents, or that he should have been taken with his brother. Actually, he wished that last bit had happened, but he suspected he wouldn't have been left with Toby. There could only be a few reasons why Toby had been taken, and it would no doubt have been more lucrative for his kidnappers to separate them if they'd been together.

But they hadn't been. Sam had escaped into the forest, and when he'd gone back home—

No. he wasn't going to think about that. He wasn't sure what was happening today that he couldn't stop thinking about the past, but it was never a good thing. He had to focus on eating and drinking, and on deciding where he was going to spend the night. The house was probably too far, but maybe he could at least head that way. He could be there tomorrow and spend a few days before he had to go back out to find food again.

A sound made him look up, his heart beating faster. He prayed it was a bunny, or maybe a squirrel, but of course, he wasn't that lucky. He never was.

A wolf was standing on the other side of the stream, staring at Sam. It didn't move, and it wasn't threatening, but that didn't mean it wouldn't try to eat Sam, so Sam stepped back.

The wolf rose on its hind legs and became a man.

Sam was used to shifters—he was one after all, just like his entire family had been—but that didn't make the shock easier to deal with. The fact that a wolf shifter was there meant he'd strayed too close to town and the pack that lived close by. He couldn't afford *anyone* knowing about him.

"Don't leave. Please," the wolf shifter said. He raised his hands and showed them to Sam as if that would be enough for Sam to know he wasn't dangerous.

But he was. Men, people, always were. That was one of the reasons Sam's parents had kept their family isolated. They would have been torn apart and used otherwise—and they *had* been.

"I'm not going to hurt you. God, you're beautiful."

Sam resisted the urge to preen. He knew he was gorgeous in his shifted form. His kind always was. That wasn't why they were hunted, of course, but it didn't mean he wasn't proud of it, especially after living in the forest on his own for so long.

"Can I come closer?" the wolf asked.

That was enough to snap Sam back to reality. He should have been more careful. Who knew what was going to happen to him if the pack found out he was in the forest? He could imagine it all too well. They'd capture him and lock him up, use him and make him miserable. He might not have a lot to be grateful or happy for in his life, but he was free, and that was something, even though he wished he were dead sometimes.

"I promise I won't hurt you," the wolf said.

Sam couldn't believe him. The only people he would have believed were either dead or gone, and he couldn't afford to risk his life, no matter how much he longed for human contact.

It had been so long since he'd heard another person talk, since he'd last been touched. He wanted his mother's caresses back, his father's gruff voice back. He wanted to allow the wolf to cuddle him and to tell him everything was going to be okay.

Instead of staying where he was and giving the wolf a chance to touch him, he turned around and galloped away.

His heart was racing, and not because he was running. He'd been close to the pack, too close—closer than he'd ever allowed himself to come since his family had been destroyed. What did it mean? Was the pack going to hunt him now that they knew he was there? He'd probably encroached on their territory, so they'd be in their right to do so. They could come into the forest and hunt him, and he wouldn't be able to do anything. He couldn't even defend himself, not against wolves. He wasn't a predator.

He was prey. His entire family had been, and things hadn't gone well for them. He didn't want to think about it, but he doubted things would go well for him, either.

Sam ran until he was out of breath. He wasn't sure where he was when he stopped, but a bit of sniffing around confirmed he was far away from the wolf and his pack, closer to his home. He should have smelled the place when he'd reached the stream, but he'd been so thirsty. He was still hungry, too, and he wasn't sure what food he'd be able to find at home. There wasn't much in the house itself, but he could walk around for a bit and try to find some grass. He needed some time for his heart to slow down anyway, and he wasn't looking forward to going inside the house.

It wasn't a home anymore. It hadn't been in a while, not since his parents had been killed and his brother taken. Sam hadn't been able to walk away from it yet, though. He wasn't sure he ever would be, not when it was the only thing that still tied him to his family.

He headed toward the house. The people who'd killed his parents had set it on fire before leaving, and the fire had destroyed about half of the house before dying out. Sam knew he should be glad for the rain that night, but he wasn't sure he was. The house was like a tether that kept him coming back even though he knew he shouldn't. It was the only thing he still had from his family, and leaving it and the forest behind wasn't something Sam wanted to consider.

Besides, the world outside the forest was dangerous for him. The people who'd killed his parents and taken his brother wouldn't think twice about grabbing him, too, and neither would most people who recognized him for what he was. They'd want to use him like they were no doubt using Toby, and while Sam wanted nothing more than to find his brother and take him home, he knew he'd get caught. He didn't have the skills to find his brother. Besides, what would he bring Toby back to?

Their family was gone. The house they'd grown up in was

gone. What was left was a half burned down house and two graves. The forest was only relatively safe, what with the town and the pack being close enough that it only took a few hours of running to get there. Sam should have been more careful where he was going, but it was so easy to lose track of time and of where he was when he was in his shifted form.

Would the wolf come after him now that he knew he was there? Sam hoped he wouldn't, but he knew better. He was precious, especially for other shifters who knew what he could do. He might have been safe from a human who wouldn't have understood what they were seeing, but from a shifter who knew Sam wasn't just a legend?

Sam was going to have to be more careful like he had right after he'd lost his family.

A unicorn shifter. Frederic couldn't believe what he'd seen, what he'd *smelled.* His mate was a unicorn shifter, and he didn't know where to start with that.

He'd come to the stream to drink before going back to the pack. They used this part of the forest to run, and it was part of the pack's territory. That was why he hadn't expected to find anyone there, at least not someone he didn't know.

Where had his mate come from? Frederic didn't know much about unicorn shifters. They were beautiful, of course, and their horn was rumored to have healing proprieties. That was why they'd been hunted to near extinction.

Was Frederic's mate alone in the forest, or did he have a family with him? Was that why he was hiding? He'd been frightened, although that might have as much to do with the fear of being hunted than the shock or being found when he hadn't expected it.

Did he even know Frederic was his mate, though?

Frederic was a wolf, so he had a strong sense of smell. He didn't know what kind of smell unicorn shifters could catch, though. Had Frederic's mate run away because he was afraid Frederic would hurt him because he hadn't recognized him as his mate? Or had he, and then run because he didn't want Frederic?

Frederic had no way of knowing, and he didn't particularly want to think about the second possibility. He was going to have to ask his mate and to do that, he needed to find him first.

Where should he start? His mate had to live somewhere in the forest. Frederic didn't know about anyone new in town, although he might just not have heard about it. He'd have to ask. But His mate had smelled of the forest and not of the town and humans. In fact, he'd barely smelled human at all. Now that Frederic thought about it, he'd only detected one human scent on his mate, and it had to belong to him. There hadn't been others, which might indicate that Frederic's mate was on his own. He certainly didn't have regular contact with other people, because Frederic would have been able to tell.

What was his mate doing all alone in the forest? There was only one way for Frederic to find out, and it was to go after his mate. He couldn't just run, though. He needed to talk to the alpha and his family, tell them he wasn't going to be around. He already knew Alpha Cook wouldn't try to stop him from going into the forest, but he needed to know there was a unicorn shifter so close to town and the pack. Frederic didn't think for one moment that his mate was dangerous, but others were, and some people wouldn't stop for anything to get their hands on a unicorn's horn. Since Frederic hoped his mate would eventually move in with him in pack territory, that meant the pack might be in danger.

He rubbed his face. He wasn't sure how long he'd been

standing there staring at the spot where his mate had disappeared, but he needed to move. He had no way to be sure his mate would stay in the forest. He might have been there just to run and to let his unicorn out. What if he'd already gone back to his car and was driving away? Frederic didn't think so, but he couldn't be sure.

He shifted again and ran back toward the houses in which the pack lived. The pack wasn't big, just over thirty members, and their houses were close to each other. They all lived there rather than in town with humans, but then, they were a pack. Frederic didn't have anything against humans. He even liked most of them. But they'd never understand what being a shifter meant, and that was okay. They didn't have to understand, just to accept that shifters were a part of the world.

Frederic meant to go straight to Alpha Camden Cook's house, but of course, he was sidetracked when he reached the pack. Reece was outside his house, under the car he'd been fixing for the past few years, and Frederic couldn't *not* tell him what had just happened. They were best friends, and he knew Reece would be happy for him and would probably offer to go with him to help find his mate.

Frederic climbed Reece's porch and shifted. He opened the chest Reece kept there and took out a set of his clothes. He kept changes of clothes on his porch, on Reece's, on his parents', and on his sister's. That way he could dress wherever he happened to be when he shifted.

"I thought you'd gone for a run," Reece said. He slid out of under the car and was on his feet, attempting to clean his hands with a rag.

"I did," Frederic said before sticking his head into a t-shirt.

"And you're already done?"

"Something happened." Frederic dug into the chest for

shoes. He dumped the first pair he found back in because they weren't his.

"Something happened? What? Are you okay?"

Frederic smiled. "Yeah, I am." Trust Reece's mind to go straight to bad things happening. He worried too much. Frederic always told him that, but he never changed, and that was one of the reasons everyone loved him.

Reece rolled his eyes. "What is it, then? Or are you going to let me worry myself to death."

Frederic closed the chest and sat onto it to put his shoes on. He wasn't sure how to say it. Finding his mate was great news, of course, but he knew Reece's situation, so he wasn't sure how to tell him without hurting him.

He licked his lips. "There was someone at the stream when I stopped there."

"Someone from the pack?"

"No." Frederic hesitated.

Reece noticed it, of course. "Just get out with it, Freddy. I want to help if something is wrong, and if everything's okay like you're saying, I want to, I don't know, celebrate with you."

Frederic breathed out. He was going to have to tell Reece about this sooner or later anyway, and Reece would be hurt if he wasn't one of the first to find out. "There was a shifter at the stream. A unicorn shifter."

Reece sucked in a breath. "A unicorn?"

"Yeah. I couldn't believe it when I first saw him. But that's not all."

"I kinda hate you right now, Freddy. Come on. Did the unicorn talk to you? Did he try to stab you with his horn or something?"

Frederic snorted. Unicorns were rare, but he doubted any of them were aggressive. They were too beautiful to be bloodthirsty. Right? "No. But I could smell him. He's my mate."

Reece's eyes widened. There were a lingering sadness and pain there, but there was also shock and happiness. "You're serious."

"Of course I am. I wouldn't play around with this."

"Where is he, then?" Reece looked around as if Frederic's mate might burst out of the forest. Frederic wished he would, but of course, he had no such luck.

His mate was far away, but hopefully, he was still in the forest. "He ran away."

Reece blinked. "What did you do?"

"Nothing."

"You said something, then?"

Frederic punched Reece's shoulder. "Shut up, asshole. I didn't do anything. I just shifted and tried to talk to him. He was spooked, though."

"And you didn't go after him?"

"Trust me, I wanted to, but I think I need to talk to Camden first. He needs to know there's a unicorn around, especially if my mate is going to become a pack member."

Reece grimaced. "Right. Well, go see him, then, and let me know if there's anything I can do to help you."

"I will." Frederic turned to leave. His gaze caught Sage's, who was sitting on his porch doing something that might have been cleaning vegetables. Frederic waved at him, and he waved back. Frederic looked at Reece, already knowing what he'd find, and sure enough, Reece's cheeks were red, and he was carefully avoiding looking at Sage.

Frederic wanted to say something, and he would have any other time. He had something to do now, though.

He could push Reece about Sage and his love life later, once he had his mate with him.

The house was like Sam had left it.

There wasn't much left of the roof, the tiles and everything else having burned away. A part if it was still there, but it wasn't much, just enough for Sam to be able to spend the night there when it rained and he didn't feel like sleeping under the water in his unicorn form.

The half of the house where the roof was gone was in pretty much the same state. The walls were still standing, but they were black with soot and burn marks. The windows on that side were broken, the glass dimly glinting in the light that made it through the trees. Sam's father had taken care of cutting down the trees and bushes around the house when they'd all still been there, but Sam spent most of his time in his unicorn form. He didn't need much light, not even when he was home.

He made his way inside, taking care not to catch his mane on anything. He'd long ago cleaned up a path to the room he used the most in the house. It had been his parents' bedroom, and it was located downstairs. Part of the internal wall was gone, burned with the rest, but the outside one was still sturdy, and Sam had cleaned up as much as he'd been able to. He didn't like spending time there, not with the memories that haunted his mind every time he was there, but it was nice to be relatively warm during the winter.

He shifted and pushed open the door he always kept closed. The last thing he wanted was for animals to come in and use his room, although that hadn't happened yet. They could smell he wasn't just human, and they respected him—or they feared him. He wasn't sure which, and he didn't care.

He left the door open and grabbed the clothes he'd left on the dresser. He quickly put them on and tried not to frown at the feeling of clothes on his skin. He'd been spending too much time in his unicorn form again. He knew that, but it was easier to wander around the forest as a unicorn. It also made ignoring the pain and the sadness that still lingered in his mind easier.

Once he was dressed, he went through his routine. He always made a round of the house when he first got there. He stopped in the kitchen and gently touched the frames hanging on the walls, looking at his parents' smiles, and his brother's grimaces. Sometimes, he had a hard time remembering how happy they'd been. They'd been extremely isolated, but they'd been safe and together. Sam hadn't always been happy at not being able to leave the forest, but he'd understood why his parents wanted to keep him and Toby there. Even they didn't leave often, yet it had been enough for someone in town to realize what they were and come looking for them.

He paused in front of a portrait of his mother and couldn't help but smile. She wasn't there anymore, but he still loved her. "Hey, Mom."

She didn't answer, of course. No one did. The forest around the house was quieter than anywhere else, making Sam feel like he was an island. No one would disturb him. No one would think he was weird or crazy for talking to his dead mother.

"I met someone today. I know it's weird. I mean, it's not like I go out of my way to meet new people, or people, period. I didn't mean to get so close to the pack. It's dangerous, and it was terrifying. But somehow, I can't bring myself to regret it completely."

He left the portrait behind and went to sit in his mother's chair. He'd moved a lot of stuff to the kitchen table, and it had become a small altar for his family. There were other pictures there, and small objects his parents and his brother had loved. He picked up the cat figurine his mom had favored and ran his thumb over the smooth surface while his thoughts went back to the wolf.

"He's a wolf shifter. I don't know anything about him. I didn't give him time to say much." Sam snorted. "I freaked out. He's the first guy I've ever seen, well, you know, and I ran away. I can't even be sure he would have hurt me. I know Dad would say I did the right thing if he knew, but I'm not sure. I've been alone for a long time, you know? And I kind of wish I had someone to talk to sometimes." Sam paused. "Well, someone who'd answer me."

Sam wondered what his mom would have told him about it. His father would have been cautious and careful, just in case the wolf wanted to use Sam and his horn or to sell him, but his mom wasn't as disillusioned.

She would have told Sam to follow his heart.

Sam couldn't be sure, but he'd talked to his mom about mates plenty of times. His parents had been mates, and they'd been happy together. They'd never fought, only bickered over stupid things, and they'd never spent any length of time away from the other after they'd met. Sam had grown up watching them, and he'd yearned for that kind of love and acceptance, that kind of care only a mate could give him.

He knew from his mother that once you met your mate, you couldn't stop thinking about him or her, that they became the center of your universe, and that any plan you made after that happened, it included them.

That would explain why he couldn't get the wolf out of his mind. Sam hadn't realized it at the time, but he must have smelled the wolf. That would have been enough to tell his unicorn they were mates. The fact that he'd freaked out before pausing to examine his feelings didn't change the fact that the wolf could be his mate. He didn't have a way to make sure of that, of course. That would imply going to the pack to find the wolf, and there was no way Sam was going to do that, no matter how tempted he was.

He didn't know the wolf or even the pack. He'd been taught to stay away from them, and he had. He was lonely, though. He'd always had someone in his life. Even when he fought with his parents, he'd had Toby. But now, he'd been alone for a long time, and he yearned for that to change.

Could he trust the wolf he thought was his mate, though? How was he supposed to let go of the fear and the distrust and let the wolf into his life? He'd never done anything like that. He'd never even thought about it. As stupid as it was, he'd thought he'd be on his own in the forest for the rest of his life. He was only in his early twenties, though. He wasn't sure how much time had passed since his parents had been killed, and he didn't want to find out. He was going to if he wanted to let the wolf into his life, though.

But again, how could he trust the wolf or his pack?

Sam put the cat figurine down. The only way for him to find out if the man he thought was his mate and his people were trustworthy would be to observe them. If they didn't know what he was, they'd behave like they normally did, and Sam would be able to tell if they were good people or if they'd sell his ass and his horn to the best offer.

That meant leaving the house and the forest where Sam felt safe, though. He could spy on the pack from the edge of the forest, either in his human form or in his unicorn one, but still. He wouldn't have the relative safety of the house if something happened. He had no way to be sure he'd ever come back. What would happen to the house and the things in it if he was captured and sold?

He'd have to be careful. He couldn't think about not going, though. He felt like he'd met his future this morning, and he wanted to know if he was right, if that was what had happened. And the only way to get that was to put himself out there and go to observe the pack.

Frederic knocked on the alpha's door. Camden always said his house was open to everyone and to walk in without knocking, but Frederic wouldn't have appreciated it if people did that at his house, so he preferred to knock. Being the alpha didn't mean Camden had to give up his privacy.

The door opened. Camden was wearing an apron that was dirty with flour and what had to be chocolate because the air in his house smelled like cookies. He grinned at Frederic and waved him inside. "Come in. I was just looking for someone to try my cookies."

Frederic wanted to blurt everything out and go back to the forest, but he also had to go to his parents' house to tell them what was going on, and he *was* kind of hungry. Besides, Camden was a great baker, and Frederic didn't want to miss his cookies.

He followed Camden to the kitchen. Camden was pretty much what one would expect from an alpha—tall, wide shoulders, arms bulging with muscles. His blond hair was cut short, and he had brown eyes that most people described as the color of chocolate. Frederic just thought they were brown, and they sometimes looked like he wanted to kill people with his gaze. He probably did, actually. Their pack was small, but they had to deal with the people in town, and some of them were idiots.

"Sit down. Do you want a glass of milk to go with the cookies?" Camden asked.

Frederic was nervous, but he nodded. He wasn't sure what Camden would think about him having a unicorn mate. He'd be over the moon about Frederic finding his mate, that was obvious. He'd never cared about what mates were before, or who, but Frederic's mate came with complications that other people didn't have to deal with.

Camden put a plate full of cookies in front of Frederic. He opened the fridge and took out the milk. "So, what are you here for? Not that I don't appreciate the company, but I'm sure you have better things to do on Sundays than hanging around with me."

Frederic wrapped his hands around his glass of milk. "I went for a run earlier."

"Yeah? That's nice. Or did something happen?"

"Are there unicorn shifters in the woods?"

Camden blinked and sat in front of Frederic. "Unicorn shifters?"

"Yes. I, well, I went to the stream to drink after I ran, and there was a unicorn. He's also my mate, so . . . ." Frederic just threw everything out there. He might as well.

Camden leaned back in his chair. "Well, shit. You don't do things by half, do you?"

"It's not like I chose him as my mate."

"I know, I know. And I'm happy for you. You know I don't care that your mate is a guy or even that he's a unicorn shifter. I'm not the kind of man who will try to use him. Not everyone will see things the way I do, though."

"I realize that. That's why I wanted to tell you before I went back to the forest. He didn't seem happy to see me, and he ran. I'm not even sure he knows we're mates."

"Well, there *was* a rumor that a unicorn family lived around here. I can't tell you much about them, though. They kept to themselves, and I can't blame them for that. It means I'm not sure of anything, though, not even that they actually exist. Although since you've seen at least one of them, maybe the rumors are true."

"Maybe." Frederic hadn't thought about what his mate's presence in the forest meant. Where had he come from? Frederic would have found him sooner if he'd visited the town, even only a few times. So maybe he wasn't from around here. The only way for Frederic to find out would be to talk to his mate, and he couldn't wait.

Camden tapped his fingertips on the table. "This is going to complicate things for us."

"I know. I'm sorry."

Camden shrugged. "Don't be. It's not like you chose him, and there has to be a reason he of all people is your mate. Besides, at least the pack isn't going to try to take advantage of him. We're going to have to be more careful, though, maybe hire some security. I'll do that right now. We might as well start as soon as possible."

Frederic rubbed his face. He hated causing so much trouble. The pack had never needed security. No one bothered them usually, but Camden was right. If people found out they had a unicorn member, they'd try to get him, so the pack needed to be prepared. Frederic would have been surprised Camden wasn't saying *no* if he hadn't known his alpha. "Thank you."

"No worries. I suppose you have things to do, so go. Just make sure to bring your mate around once you find him, okay? I'd like to talk to him and reassure him. He'll probably need it."

Frederic pressed his lips together. "We could leave. I mean, you don't *have* to welcome my mate into the pack, and if us leaving keeps everyone else safe—"

"No." Camden leaned forward. "You've been a pack member since you were a kid. We grew up together. I'm not going to kick you out because you met your mate."

"It would be easier."

Camden grinned. "Since when do we do things the easy way? No. We'll do the *right* thing, not the easy one. That means that your mate is welcome here, as much as you are. That is, if you ever go get him."

Frederic grinned. He hadn't really thought Camden

would want him to leave. They were friends, and like Camden had said, they'd grown up together. Besides, Camden did do the right thing rather than the easy one most of the time. "I'll be back when I'm back."

"I'll make sure no one worries. But I want to see you in a few days, whether you've found him or not. I don't want anything to happen to you while you're away."

"I'll come around, then."

Frederic left Camden to his cookies—which were delicious, especially with milk—and went to his house. There wasn't much for him to do. He called work and told them he wasn't going to come for a few days, made sure there was nothing around that could go bad while he wasn't home, and called his parents. He could have gone to their house, but it was easier this way. His mom would have tried to coddle him and make sure he brought a bag of food and whatever else she thought he might need, but he didn't want to do that. He was a wolf. He could hunt if he needed to.

He couldn't know how long he'd need to stay in the forest. He'd have to come back every few days to let Camden and his family know he was okay, but there was no way for him to know if his mate would bolt the next time he saw him or if he'd realized they were mates and he'd be looking for him. Frederic didn't mind spending time as a wolf, but he liked his comforts. He wasn't looking forward to sleeping on the ground, not even in his wolf form. He also liked running water and to be able to watch hockey on his giant screen TV.

He looked around his house and tried to imagine his mate living there with him. He didn't even know what his mate looked like. Was he blond, maybe almost white, like his mane was in his unicorn form? Or did he have dark hair? What about his eyes? Were they dark or light? Was he tall or on the short side? What did he like? Would he even want to move in with Frederic, or would he prefer Frederic go live wherever he lived?

All of those were questions Frederic couldn't wait to find answers to, but he needed to stop worrying and thinking about them. He had to find his mate. That was the only way he'd get those answers.

He didn't lock his front door—no one ever did—when he left the house. He stripped on his porch and stuffed his clothes into the bench he had there for that reason.

When he shifted, he howled. His wolf pushed, wanting them to find their mate and bring him home.

Frederic hopped off the porch and ran.

Chapter Two

Sam wasn't sure how much time had passed since he'd found his mate at the stream. A few days, at the very least. He tended to lose track of time when he was in his unicorn form, though.

He'd been hanging around the forest close to the pack since he'd left the house, but so far, he hadn't seen his mate. He remembered him and the way he looked, so he was sure of that.

Now that he'd had time to think about what was happening, Sam realized this was probably not the best way to meet his mate again. He'd been carrying a bag with the clothes he usually used when he was in his human form, but they were old, and they hadn't been washed since the last time his mom had done it for him. Sam also hadn't taken a shower since then. He bathed in the streams in the forest every so often, but he didn't use soap, so he probably didn't smell too good.

Should he go into town and buy new clothes? He'd brought some soap with him, just in case, but where was he supposed to use it? He could probably get a room in a motel in town or something, if he had enough money. He wasn't sure how much it would cost, so he couldn't be sure the money he'd found in the house after his parents had died would be enough for both clothes and a room.

He could probably buy clothes, though. He didn't want to meet his mate wearing rags. He also didn't want to go into town, though. He couldn't remember the last time he'd been there, but it had been when his parents had still been around. He'd gone with his father, and he remembered a large store that seemed to sell pretty much anything, from pet food to clothes, to food. Things were no doubt different now, and Sam wasn't looking forward to being around people, not when he couldn't be sure if they were trustworthy. He hoped most of the people would be humans, but he had no way to be sure of that. What if he met a shifter and they decided to take him?

Sam licked his lips and peered between the trees. The place where the pack lived was nice. Most of the houses were arranged in a loose circle, with a big fire pit in the middle. Benches circled it, and it was obviously a place where the pack enjoyed spending time together.

Sam didn't know which house belonged to his mate, or he'd have moved closer to it.

But no. He needed to be decently clean when he met his wolf, and he wasn't right now. That meant going to town.

Sam wasn't sure he was ready, but since he needed to do it, he might as well go now. He didn't like the thought of leaving pack territory, which was ridiculous since he wasn't a pack member, but he'd felt safe in the few days he'd been hanging around there.

He trotted as close to town as he dared in his unicorn form, keeping to the forest and making sure no one could see him. Once he was close enough that he could walk the rest of the distance as a human, he shifted and quickly dressed. No one would probably think anything of a naked guy in the woods, not with the pack being so close to town, but still. He didn't fancy having people seeing him naked. It made him feel vulnerable, and he'd already had plenty of that in his life.

Sam wrinkled his nose as he pulled on the clothes. The sweater was too large, and it had a suspicious looking stain on the front. He rubbed at it, but it had to be old, and he knew he wouldn't get it out of the fabric.

His jeans were better, even though they were too large. He knew that would be the case, though, so he'd brought a belt. He pulled it as tight as he could, then put his shoes on without socks. He couldn't do much for his hair, and he tied it back as neatly as he could.

Then he was ready to face the town.

He didn't feel like it, but then, he'd expected that. He was going to have to get used to being with people if he wanted any kind of relationship with his mate, though. He couldn't imagine the wolf would be eager to move into the forest with him. The house wasn't inhabitable, not to anyone but Sam, and Sam didn't want to take his mate away from his family and his pack. He already knew he'd have to move there, and he was ready to do it. He just had to get used to being around people again.

Sam took a deep breath and made his way out of the forest. He wasn't sure where to go once he was on the sidewalk, so he looked around. He thought he remembered the store being close to the forest, so he was relieved when he noticed a parking lot on his left. He walked toward it, smiling a bit when he recognized the store. It was the same as it had been the last time he'd been there, although he thought the name above the door had changed. It didn't matter, though. The store was as big as it had been, so he knew he'd be able to find clothes there.

Once inside, he made sure to select clothes he could afford, adding the numbers a few times so he knew he had enough money. His shoes would do, so he only picked a pair of jeans and a new sweater. He wondered about socks and underwear and decided to buy a pair of both. He didn't care that the socks had avocado halves printed on them. He just needed his feet to be comfortable in his shoes.

He paid, his heart racing as he prayed the woman at the check-out wouldn't recognize him as a unicorn shifter. She didn't look happy with him, but that was probably more because of how dirty he was than because of what he was. He gave her a tight smile and promised himself he'd find a way to shower. He had to. He didn't want his mate to be disgusted by him.

Sam shoved his new clothes into his backpack and swung it onto his back. He left the store and looked around for a motel he might be able to get a room at, but stopped when he noticed a group of men at the back of the parking lot.

Three bigger men were circling a smaller one. The smaller one looked fragile, and Sam thought he also looked scared. Sam didn't blame him, not with the three mountains intended on hurting him.

Sam swallowed. What should he do? He didn't like the thought of leaving this guy to fend for himself—not when he looked like he wouldn't be able to—but getting involved in this would mean being more vulnerable to discovery. He couldn't tell if the men attacking the smaller one were shifters or humans, not from where he was.

He made his decision a second later when he saw one of the big men grab the smaller one by the arm and pull him forward. Sam ran toward them, yelling, "Let him go!"

It probably wasn't smart, but it worked. The man dropped his hand, and the smaller one backed away toward his car. His eyes were wide, yet he didn't climb into his car to leave. He stayed there and watched Sam move closer.

Sam stopped by the car. "Leave him alone."

"Who the fuck do you think you are?" one of the big men asked with a sneer.

"No one. But leave him alone."

"See, that's none of your business. Unless, of course, you *want* to make it your business, in which case we'll be more than happy to pound your ass into the ground like we're about to do with the faggot here."

Sam's entire body flushed with heat. He hated bullies. He hated people who found hurting vulnerable people fun. He hated them because they'd been the people who'd hurt his family, who'd taken his parents from him and were still holding Toby. They weren't these guys in particular, but they were all the same, thinking everyone else should cater to them.

Sam didn't even realize he was shifting until one of the guys gasped. He didn't have the time to shift back or to hide his horn, though, so he charged the trio, intent on stabbing them with the horn. The damn thing might as well be useful in this case—it had brought Sam so much sorrow.

But the trio didn't even allow him to get close. They turned and ran before Sam could touch them, and though he wanted to run after them, he shifted back to his human form. The fewer people who saw him, the better it would be.

"You tore your clothes," a soft voice said.

Sam wrapped his arms around himself. "That's fine. I have more." He didn't have other shoes, but he probably had enough money to buy a cheap pair.

The small man stopped in front of Sam. He was holding a blanket, and Sam accepted it with a smile. "Thank you."

"You helped me. You don't need to thank me." He licked his lips. "I'm Sage. You're a unicorn."

Sam winced. "Yeah."

"It's okay. Why don't I go get you some shoes? You can dress and wait in my car."

"I should go."

"Please. I know you're worried about what I could do, but it's obvious I wouldn't be able to hurt you even if I tried, and I promise you the pack will only thank you for helping me."

Sam's heart beat harder. "You live with the pack?"

"Yes."

Sam supposed this was one way to find his mate.

Frederic was frustrated. He could smell his mate in the forest, under the scent of the trees, the rotting leaves on the ground, the small animals who lived there, and other shifters, but he hadn't been able to find him yet.

It didn't make sense. It was obvious by now that Frederic's mate was hanging around the edge of the forest close to the pack. He was probably watching the pack, so it gave Frederic hope that he'd realized they were mates. Why couldn't he smell that Frederic was looking for him, though?

The fact that Frederic's mate was repeatedly hanging around the same spots meant his scent was muddled, and Frederic hadn't been able to follow it to his mate yet. He hoped he would, because he'd had enough of the forest, even though it had only been two days. He wanted a shower and his bed, dammit.

Maybe he should leave the area around the pack and go deeper in to the forest. His mate had spent a lot of time by the pack, but Frederic had caught his scent on a few different trails, and they all led away from the pack. It might help him if he followed one of them. It wasn't like he was making any progress anyway.

Frederic raised his nose and sniffed. He could smell his mate—he was familiar with his scent now—and he followed the trail deeper in the forest. The scent grew fainter, so he knew his mate hadn't been there in a few days, but he was curious to see where his mate lived, and maybe the trail would lead him there.

It did. Frederic hadn't expected what he found, though. He'd suspected his mate lived in the forest somewhere, maybe with his family since Camden had said a family lived around there, but what he found was a burned down house. It was empty from what he could hear and smell, and he knew the fire had happened a while back. He didn't go in, though. This was his mate's home, no matter the state it was in, and he didn't want to invade it.

He sat in front of the house and looked at it. He could see signs of the people who'd once lived there. There was a mostly rotten book on the porch, next to a pair of boots. A shovel had been abandoned by the porch steps, almost as if whoever had left it there was about to come back and pick it up again. There were still curtains on the windows of the part of the house that hadn't burned, and the shock of their cheerful design hit Frederic right in the guts.

Was this really where his mate still lived? How could he stand to be around the house? Frederic suspected that the fact that his mate was still in the forest meant he'd lost the rest of his family, and that he was alone in this shell of a house—alone with the memories. Frederic's heart hurt for him, even though he didn't know anything about the circumstances of the fire.

Frederic shook himself. His mate wasn't in the house or anywhere around it, and being there without him felt like a break of trust even though they'd never talked. He hoped his mate would take him here again once they were together and he trusted him, but for now, he needed to leave.

He trotted back between the trees. He might as well go back to pack territory and try to find his mate's trail again. He hated that he didn't even know his mate's name. He wanted to think of him as a human being, but he couldn't, not yet. He didn't care what kind of shifter his mate was, even though he knew most people would. The only reason it mattered to him was that he knew unicorn shifters were hunted and that he was going to have to find a way to keep his mate safe.

That was, if he ever managed to find him.

He huffed and followed his mate's trail back to the pack. It took him a while to get there, and when he did, he walked around the territory, trying to find a more recent trail. His mate had to be somewhere.

But he wasn't around the pack, and Frederic wanted to hit his head on the closest tree trunk. He couldn't continue searching the forest. It hadn't worked until now, and he doubted it would. Where else could his mate be, then?

In town? Frederic wasn't sure about that, but he might as well give it a try. He could go there in his wolf form, sniff around, and see what he found. It would be easier for him to find a trail as a wolf, and he'd be faster, too.

He headed toward town. He might miss his couch and his well-stocked kitchen, but it was nice to be in the forest and be able to run around without having to think about what time it was or what he still had to do before the day was over. His boss had been great about giving him time off, but he was going to have to go back sooner or later. Hopefully, he'd do so once he'd found his mate and things had settled between them.

Frederic didn't know what to expect from his mate and the relationship they'd build together. He didn't even know if his mate wanted him. He wasn't worried about the way his mate had run away when they'd first met, but still. His mate hadn't come back. Or maybe he had, in a way. There had to be a reason he was sticking close to the pack. He'd never done that before, because someone would have smelled him. So it was new, and it *had* to have to do with Frederic.

Or at least that was what Frederic was trying to convince himself of.

He left the forest and trotted along the sidewalk. Shifters didn't usually go into town in their animal forms, but it happened, and no one was scared or scandalized by it. A few humans looked at Frederic with a scowl, but he ignored them. There would always be humans who didn't like shifters and shifters who didn't like humans. He wasn't one of those, and he'd learned a while ago not to let what others thought get to him.

He froze when he caught a tendril of scent. He'd recognize it anywhere since he'd been hunting it for the past two days, and this was the strongest he'd found it until now.

He followed it to the main store. It separated in the parking lot, the weakest trail going to the store and probably inside, the strongest one staying in the back of the parking lot—so that was where Frederic went.

He frowned when he smelled other people. Two—no, three—men he didn't know, and Sage. Sage's scent mixed with the one Frederic knew was his mate's enough that he thought they'd probably talked and spent some time together. The fact that they also disappeared more or less in the same spot made him think they might have left together, probably in Sage's car.

What was Sage doing with Frederic's mate? Where had he taken him? Frederic trusted Sage. He'd trust him with his life, and he certainly wasn't jealous, but he was curious and worried, and yes, he wished his mate had chosen him to trust and to shift with. Because there was no way his mate had climbed into Sage's car in his unicorn form, which meant he'd shifted and that Sage probably knew more about him than Frederic right now.

Frederic huffed. *Right.* Who cared who knew what about his mate? The important thing was that Frederic's mate was safe, and that he probably was already in pack territory.

Frederic had to find Sage.

He ran back to the pack, his thoughts filled with his mate. He felt like his life was about to change, to tilt one way or another. He didn't know which way it would go, but he was about to find out.

Sam looked around. It had been a while since he'd last been in a real house, or one without half of it burned down. He'd never been to a friend's house, either. He'd been homeschooled, and he hadn't had friends. He still didn't.

Sage put the bags of groceries on the table in the kitchen. "Feel free to look around," he said with a smile.

Sam nodded, but he didn't move. He wasn't going to stick his nose in stuff that wasn't his. Would Sage be offended, though? God, Sam wished he knew how to do this. He hated feeling insecure, probably because he'd felt that way for the past few years.

But Sage just smiled at him and started taking things out of the bags. "This pack is nice, you know. I'm an outsider, too, but they didn't think twice about taking me in."

"Really?" Sam wanted to sit down, but he didn't want to get Sage's chairs dirty. He still had to shower. He was even more aware of it after the ride in Sage's car.

"Really. And I'm sure you'll be welcome, too."

Sam snorted softly. Of course he would be. Everyone would want him. Having a unicorn shifter was a commodity.

Sage shook his head. "I know what you're thinking, but that's not it. Camden—Alpha Cook—is a good man. He'd never take advantage of you or what you can do. He's not that kind of person."

Sam shrugged. He'd thought that he might want to be part of the pack, but he knew better. "Even if he really is like that, I'd bring the pack a lot of trouble. People are ready to do anything to get to me."

Sage grimaced. "I see. And you think that if people found

out you were here, they'd try to take you?"

"I know they would. They took my brother."

Sage looked like he might be about to cry. Sam wasn't sure why, but he didn't know what to do with someone who cried, not someone he barely knew. So he looked around again, both to give Sage time to compose himself and because he was curious. "This is nice."

Sage cleared his throat. "It is. And I'm sure the pack would find a way to work things out if you decided to stay with us. Why were you in town earlier? Or would you rather not tell me? Because that's okay, too."

Sam wasn't sure what to do. He wanted to tell Sage about his mate, but shouldn't he, well, find his mate first? He suspected the wolf had told people about him—he'd have had to, considering Sam was a unicorn—but the people here were his friends and his family. Sam had no one like that he could talk to.

Sage rubbed his palms on his thighs. "Okay, let's do it like this. I can see you're uncomfortable, so why don't you go get a shower? I'm sure you'd rather do that than stick around talking to me."

"I like talking to you." And Sam did. He'd been alone for too long. He hadn't even realized it until now.

Sage smiled. "That's good, because I like talking to you, too. You have a soothing presence. But I'm sure you'd like to shower, so let me show you the guest room."

Sam smiled. "Are you saying I stink?"

Sage's cheeks reddened. "Well, I wouldn't say it like that, but . . ."

Sam chuckled. "I know I do. I haven't had a shower in years. You don't have to sugarcoat the truth. I'd gone to town so I could get a room in a motel and use the bathroom."

Sam's shoulders slumped. "Oh, good. I didn't want to be

rude, but yeah, you smell."

Sam looked down at himself. "I should have bought two sets of new clothes." There was nothing wrong with the stuff he had, but he'd thought he'd be able to wash before having to put them on. Now they no doubt smelled of him, and putting them back on after his shower would be counterproductive.

Sage beamed. "See, I knew this was going to happen, so when I went back to the store to buy shoes for you, I also grabbed some clothes."

Sam blinked. "You did?"

"Yes. I hope you don't take offense, but it's obvious that you're a bit down on your luck, and I wanted to do something nice after what you did for me. You can tell me to fuck off, though."

Why would Sam do that? Sage was offering him more than he'd ever thought possible. He'd taken him home. He would allow him to shower. He'd bought him shoes and clothes. Sam wasn't sure how he'd be able to thank Sage for all of that.

He felt awkward the entire time he was in the shower, but it felt so good that he was almost able to forget about it. Not completely—he couldn't brush away the feeling that someone might burst in any second like they had the day his parents had died—so he rushed through it, but it was enough for him to feel refreshed and like a new man. Sage even gave him a brush for his hair, a toothbrush, and toothpaste, and when Sam was done, he felt better than he had in a long time. He was hungry, but he could forget about that.

He brushed his teeth and hair. It took him a while to untangle to long mass, and he wondered if he shouldn't cut it off. He probably would if he went back to live in the forest.

He almost cried when he got back to the kitchen and saw that Sage had cooked food for him. It was nothing complicated—eggs, bacon, and toast—but it felt huge to Sam anyway. "You didn't have to," he choked out.

Sage looked up from the pan in which he was stirring the eggs. "I just wanted to thank you."

"You don't have to."

"You saved me from a beating at the very least, so even if you think I don't have to, I want to. I'd be lying in a gutter if you hadn't stepped in, and we both know you put yourself at risk doing it. Word that there's a unicorn shifter in town is going to get around, and I'm sorry about that." He turned the heat off under the pan. "Sit down, Sam."

Sam obeyed. Sitting down at the table with Sage made him think of other meals, other people. Sam swallowed the tears and did his best to smile. He couldn't get his parents back, but maybe now that he had a mate and a friend, he could find his brother. He hadn't let himself think of that before because he had no way to even start that search, and he wasn't sure he did now, but he couldn't snuff out the spark of hope.

"I know this isn't easy for you," Sage said.

"I'm okay."

Sage smiled. "I'm sure you've been telling yourself that for a while. But I want you to know I was serious when I said the pack will welcome you if you choose to stay with us. You'll have to talk to Camden, of course, but I went through that process a few years ago. It's weird and awkward, but you'll be fine. And you can stay here with me for as long as you want or need to. You can have the guest room."

Sam wasn't sure what to say. His heart felt like it had climbed in his throat, and it made it hard to talk. "Thank you. Why . . . why are you doing this? You don't know me."

"You remind me of myself. I was all alone once, too. I thought I'd always be, you know? No one I found wanted me for me. I want to give back now that I have a home and a place where people love me. Besides, you need help, and I can give it to you. Why shouldn't I?"

"Thank you." What else could Sam say? He still wasn't sure he could do this, that he could trust Sage and the pack, but he was going to make a decision. He could go back to the forest and the house that was empty of everything that was important to him, or he could stick around and find out if the wolf really was his mate and if the pack could help him find Toby.

It had been a long time since he'd had to make this kind of decision, and it petrified him.

Frederic took a deep breath and knocked on Sage's door. He didn't know what or who he'd find once Sage opened, and he felt a mix of elation and nervousness he wasn't sure how to deal with. And what should he tell Sage? Should he just ask where his mate was? Would Sage even know who he was talking about?

The door opened. Frederic plastered a smile on his face and looked at Sage. "Hey."

Sage blinked. He and Frederic weren't friends, even though they were friendly. Sage always kept a bit to himself, and the fact that he'd arrived in town only a few years ago hadn't helped him. "Frederic. Hi. What can I do for you?"

"I, uh, need to talk to you?"

Sage frowned. "Is that a question?"

"No. I need to talk to you, please." Frederic didn't know if his mate was with Sage right now or if Sage had just given him a ride somewhere, and he yearned to step into the house and sniff the air.

"Sure." Sage stepped aside to let Frederic in. "Has something happened? Is Reece okay?"

That made Frederic smile. He might be focused on finding his mate, but there was no way he could miss the worry in Sage's voice. For all that Sage and Reece stayed away from each other and tried to convince themselves it was what they wanted—at least in Reece's case—it was obvious they cared for each other. Frederic wasn't going to stick his nose into that, though, not right now. He had too much on his mind. But maybe later, once he and his mate had settled down.

He didn't want to consider the option that they wouldn't.

He stepped in a took a deep breath, and there it was. His mate's scent in the air, going from the door deeper into the house. Frederic wanted to run along with it, but he didn't want to freak his mate out, and Sage deserved better than having him barge into his home like that.

"Frederic? Is Reece okay?" Sage asked, and Frederic realized he'd been so focused on his mate and his scent in the air that he hadn't answered Sage's previous question.

"He's okay." Or at least Frederic thought so. Reece wouldn't have been able to call him since he didn't have his phone with him, but he'd have shifted and come to find him if he'd needed him. Frederic hadn't even thought about grabbing his phone when he'd gone home to dress. He'd just grabbed the clothes from his porch before running to Sage's house.

Sage relaxed. "Oh. Good."

"Yes."

"What did you want, then?"

Frederic looked deeper in the house. He'd never been inside, but he knew Sage took pride in everything he did and owned. He'd seen him working with the flowers in the pots under the windows and around the porch. The inside of his house mirrored that. Everything was gleaming clean, and the air smelled of lemon and rosemary under the heavy scent of Frederic's mate.

"There's someone here with you," Frederic said. How was he supposed to ask Sage about this? Should he just blurt out that his mate was there and that he wanted to see him? He could have, but he didn't want to freak out Sage or his mate.

Sage frowned, then his expression hardened. "You need to leave Sam alone."

"Sam?" So that was Frederic's mate's name? Was it short for something, maybe Samuel? Or was he just Sam? Frederic couldn't wait to find out.

"What do you want from him, Frederic? He's a nice guy, and what he is doesn't change that. I won't let you or anyone else—"

Frederic raised his hands. "I'm not here to hurt him, Sage. And I don't care that he's a unicorn shifter. I know we're not friends, but I thought you knew that about me." And the fact that he'd jumped to the wrong conclusion so easily hurt a little.

Sage grimaced. "Sorry. I'm a bit on edge today." He rubbed his face. "It's just that some guys were dicks at the grocery store and Sam helped, so I'm a bit protective of him. He also reminds me of myself." Sage shrugged. "I'm a mess, and I don't think you'd hurt Sam or anyone else. I swear."

Frederic patted Sage's shoulder. "It's okay. Emotions run high sometimes. Can I—can I see him?"

Sage frowned. "Sam?"

"Yes. Please."

"Why?"

"Because we're mates."

Frederic snapped his head toward the sound of Sam's voice so fast his neck cracked. His mate stood there, at the entrance of whatever room he'd been in. He was watching Frederic, and he looked wary. Frederic wasn't offended by that, though. They didn't know each other. He hadn't even known Sam's name until Sage had told him.

There would be time for Sam to learn to know and trust him. The important thing was that Frederic had finally found him and that he seemed to be okay.

"Mates?" Sage said with a squeak.

Frederic swallowed. "Yes. We met in the forest a few days ago."

Sam smiled deprecatingly. "And I freaked out and ran away. How did you find me?"

"I've been looking for you since then. I came back to talk to Camden, our alpha, but I went back to the forest almost right away. I followed your scent to town, where it mingled with Sage's."

"He saved me from a beating," Sage said. He cleared his throat. "And I should probably leave the two of you alone to talk. Are you done eating, Sam, or should I put your plate in the oven?"

Sam shuffled. "Don't worry about it. I can eat it cold."

"You can, but you won't. It's no bother for me." Sage looked from Sam to Frederic. "You can use the living room, or your room if you want more privacy. I'll be in the kitchen."

Your room? Since when did Sam have a room in Sage's house? Since when did those two *know* each other?

"Thank you," Sam said in a quiet voice.

Frederic smiled at Sage and made a mental note to be extra careful when he chose a Christmas present for him this year. Actually, he could probably do something even better to thank him. Maybe he could dig a bit and see what Sage and Reece would think if being together.

But later. Right now, Frederic was going to focus on his mate.

Sam gestured toward an arch on the right side of the entrance. "The living room is that way."

Frederic followed him there, watching him and feeling a bit like a creep. He couldn't look away, though. He hadn't been able to see Sam in his human form that first time, but now he could, and he was floored.

Sam's golden-brown hair was long and damp, making Frederic wonder if it would be lighter once it was dry. His eyes were hazel, changing color every time they caught the light differently, and his nose and cheeks were dotted with freckles. He looked both adorable and incredibly hot, and that wasn't a mix Frederic was used to.

Sam was shorter than Frederic, but not by much, and he was too thin. His clothes hung on him. That didn't make him less gorgeous, although Frederic suspected he'd love the way Sam looked even if he were bald and wearing a trash bag.

He made sure to keep his distance as they walked into the living room, unwilling to spook Sam. Sam went to stand by the window, and Frederic sat down, still staring at him. "I understand why you ran," he said.

"You do?"

"I think so. I scared you. I don't know much about unicorn shifters, but I do know the thing about their horn healing. Everyone does. You're safe here, though."

"Sage already told me I was. I'm not sure if I should believe him."

There was such pain in Sam's eyes that Frederic knew something bad had happened to him. He wasn't going to ask what, though. Sam would tell him if he wanted him to know. "I want you to."

Sam was silent for a bit, and Frederic didn't push him. "You want me to stay here," he finally said.

"I hope you will, yes. The pack is where I grew up. I know everyone here. But I'll follow you if you want to leave.

That is, if you want me to go with you, of course. I'm not assuming anything right now. I know you must be confused and frightened, and that's okay. I can give you all the time and space you need." Frederic's wolf might want to make Sam theirs right away, but Frederic was also human, and he did understand that what Sam was going through was hard. "Whatever you need from me, I'll do my best to give it to you."

Frederic had never meant something as much as he meant that.

Chapter Three

Sam looked out the window and tried to imagine himself outside with the others. From Sage's living room, he could see the fire pit in the middle of pack territory perfectly, and he wasn't sure how that made him feel.

It was afternoon, so most of the people there were relaxing, playing with their kids or talking. It looked nice, and Sam wasn't used to nice anymore. He'd been hiding in Sage's house since yesterday, and he wanted to continue doing so, yet he didn't. He was a mess, and he wasn't sure how to get himself out of his funk.

He knew he could leave the house. Both Sage and Frederic had assured him of that. Even though no one there knew him, they'd sworn Sam wouldn't be attacked, and he believed them. He supposed they could both be lying to him, and he knew what had happened to his family was a big reason why he wasn't sure he should believe them, but he wanted to.

All his life, he'd only trusted his parents and his brother. Since they'd been attacked, he'd only had himself to trust. And now, well, he was opening up to other people, something he'd never thought could be possible, and it was terrifying. He had no way to know if Sage and Frederic would betray him. He didn't know them well enough to be sure of anything. He needed to trust them consciously.

"You can go out there if you want," Sage said.

He was lying on the couch reading a book. He'd told Sam he could treat the house as his own, but that was hard to do when nothing there belonged to him.

"I know." Sam sighed and looked outside again.

"But you won't. You're scared."

Sam smiled. "You've been through this, too?"

"Of course I have. I know it's not the same since you only had your family for so long, but I do understand." Sam had told Frederic and Sage what had happened to him and his family yesterday, not because he wanted their pity, but because he needed them to understand, especially Frederic.

Sam wasn't sure what he was ready for when it came to his mate. He wanted the relationship his parents had had. They'd been happy together. All of Sam's memories of them were warm and peaceful, and he had a hard time believing he could have that with Frederic.

And that was the point, wasn't it? How could he have that with Frederic if he didn't even know if he could believe him?

He finally had someone again, and he was too scared to take advantage of it.

"What's wrong?" Sage asked.

"How do you know something's wrong? We met yesterday." Sam turned around and leaned against the wall. He liked Sage, but sometimes, he was uncomfortable with him because it was as if he knew too much, as if he could read Sam.

"I can feel it."

Sam blinked. "What?"

Sage shrugged. "We can talk about this later, okay? First, tell me what's wrong."

"It's just . . . so much, yet so little." That hardly made sense even to Sam, so he tried to explain. "My life today is completely different from what it was yesterday. I was alone and spent most of my time in my unicorn form in the forest, so all these changes are huge for me, yet at the same time, I still feel as alone as I was yesterday."

"It's only been one day. You have to give yourself time to deal with everything. Not only are you here now, but you also found your mate. Anyone would be bewildered, and that's not counting everything else."

Sam tugged on his hair. Everything Sage was saying made sense, but he didn't like it. He wanted to be happy again, dammit.

Sage shuffled closer to the edge of the couch and leaned forward. "How about you try to focus on a few things that most bother you? We can talk them out and see what we come up with."

Sam sighed. He didn't want to talk, yet he wanted to because it had been so long. He was a fucking mess. "I don't know if I'm really safe here."

"Mmm, okay. I understand that, and unfortunately, it's not going to be easy to overcome that feeling. You don't know me, or Frederic, or the rest of the pack. The only way you'll be sure we're trustworthy is getting to know us, and that's going to require time."

Sam sighed. "I know."

"Maybe you could talk to Camden—I mean, he probably already knows you're here. We weren't exactly discreet yesterday when we got home, so I'm sure several people saw us, and I know Frederic probably talked to him when he realized you were his mate."

"Why hasn't he come to talk to me if he knows?"

Sage smiled. "He's giving you time. He knows you're not dangerous and that you're here because you need help. He also knows that you're here to stay, since you're Frederic's mate. He won't push you, just like Frederic isn't pushing you. That doesn't mean you shouldn't talk to him, though. Go there. Ask him how the pack works, what you can do, what he's going to do with you, what he's planning to do if someone comes looking for you. I know it might be hard to understand, but we're a pack, a family. We care for each other, and we'll make sure you're always safe."

"Because of Frederic. Because we're mates."

"For now, yes. Although I have to say I actually like you. I think you and Frederic will be good for each other, and that you'll find your place with the pack, and with him."

Sam bit his lower lip. "Will I? I don't know how to do this, Sage. Even when I still had my family, I didn't have friends. We kept to ourselves because of what we are and look how it ended. My parents are dead, and my brother is gone. I've never had friends or a boyfriend. I've never even kissed anyone! How can I be good enough for Frederic? And how can he understand me when my life has been so different from his? He has everything I don't have. He has a family, friends, the pack, a house." Sam wanted to stop talking about everything.

"You should talk to him about that, you know. He might not share your experiences, but that doesn't mean he can't understand them, and even if he can't, he can still try and be there for you. I don't know what the two of you talked about yesterday, but I know him. He's a good man."

"I think he is." Everything Sam had seen of him pointed to that.

"I *really* think you should talk to him. You're not going to get to know him if you stay here. You're not going to get to know anyone this way. I'm not saying you have to talk to everyone right now, but maybe go out? Go find Frederic and ask him to go with you when you go talk to Camden. And by the way, the sooner you do that the better it will be. People won't stop wondering and staring until they know you're here to stay and see you as a pack member, and that won't happen—"

"Until I talk to your alpha."

Sage grinned. "Exactly."

Sam was going to have to do this, wasn't he? "I'll go now."

Sage blinked. "That's not what I meant. You don't have to do everything right now. You're allowed to rest and relax after everything that's happened to you."

"I might as well get this out of the way. You're right, it won't do me any good to have one foot in and one foot out." And hopefully, once Sam was a pack member, the alpha and the pack would agree to help him find Toby and get him back.

Sam had never stopped hoping he'd find his brother, but that hope had never felt so alive. He'd never come so close, even though he was far from even knowing where Toby was.

But he wasn't alone anymore. No matter how frightened he was or how hard he found it to trust the people who were now in his life, he had to believe things would be okay. Frederic wouldn't be his mate if they weren't right for each other, and someone who would sell Sam or use him wouldn't be right for him.

He had to take that step in the dark and pray everything would work out right. It was the only way to go forward.

The knock on Frederic's door made him freeze for a moment. He always expected it to be Sam now that they both lived with the pack, but last time, it had been Reece, and before that Frederic's mother and his sister. Sam hadn't come at all yet, but it had only been one day, so Frederic wasn't despairing just yet.

He expected it to be Reece again—they ought to live together since they spent more time at each other's house than at their own—but it wasn't.

This time, it was Sam.

Frederic's heart beat faster, and he forced himself to appear calm. "Hey, Sam. I didn't expect to see you today."

Sam looked around as if he expected someone to jump him. Frederic's mom or his sister might have if they'd been around, but luckily for him, they weren't, so they wouldn't embarrass him and freak Sam out.

"I can come back another time if you're busy."

Frederic stepped aside to let Sam in. "Of course not. You can come anytime, even if I'm not home. Consider this place a second home for you." Frederic hoped it would become his only home soon, but he didn't say that. The last thing he wanted to do was to push too much and scare Sam off. He had a feeling it would be easy to do that, and that he'd lose Sam if he pushed him back into the forest.

Sam shuffled his feet. "Ah, thank you." He didn't come in, and Frederic didn't ask again. "I was talking with Sage."

He didn't continue, so Frederic asked, "What did he say?"

"That I should talk to your alpha. That I've been hiding, and that while it's understandable, I need to show people I belong here if I want them to stop staring at me." He looked around again.

Frederic realized he looked hunted. He frowned and mirrored Sam's gesture, looking around to see if anyone was actually staring at him. His house was further back from the fire pit than Sage's, but he could still see it, and while a few people were looking their way, it wasn't uncomfortable. Well, not for him anyway, but he could see why Sam wanted it to stop. "Do you want to come in?"

Sam straightened his back. "I'd rather go talk to your alpha, if that's okay. I might as well get this out of the way."

Frederic had to suppress a smile. "He's not going to eat you, you know. Camden's a good man. The worst he can do is overfeed you cookies."

Sam blinked. "Cookies?"

"Yes. He likes to bake. He says it helps him relax, and he feeds them to everyone because he can't eat them all himself." Frederic cleared his throat. "Are you sure you don't want to come in?"

Sam sighed. "I want to, yes, but I know it's because I don't want to talk to your alpha."

"Do you want me to come with you?" Frederic hoped the answer to that would be yes. He wanted to be there for Sam, and he wanted Sam to want him there.

"Would you come? I know you probably have other things to do, but I'd appreciate it."

Frederic would dump anything he was doing to go, so that wasn't a problem. "Of course I'll come. And you really shouldn't worry so much. I know it's probably a moot point to tell you that, but Camden won't do anything to you, you know."

"That's what you and Sage keep telling me."

"It's because it's true. He's young, but he's a good alpha. He had a great role model. His father was the alpha until he died five years ago, and he taught Camden well."

"But I could bring trouble to the pack because of what I am. I understand he's a good alpha, but doesn't that mean he's going to put the pack first rather than me? What's going to happen if he has to choose between the pack and me?"

There was pain in Sam's voice, but also resignation, as if he expected Camden to go the easy way and choose the pack. Frederic supposed most alphas would have done just that. Camden wasn't like most alphas, though. He wanted what was best for the pack, but he also wanted what was best for *people*. "I can't promise you anything, because it's not my place, but I know Camden. We were friends growing up. He's a few years older than me, so I always looked up to him as a big brother, and he was never one of those guys who are annoyed because their younger sibling follows them around. But what I'm trying to say is that even though you have a hard time believing it, you're part of the pack now. That means everyone will protect you. You're not alone anymore."

Sam pressed his lips together so hard they whitened.

Frederic wasn't sure what he could do to make him feel better. He knew Sam would need time to get used to living with a pack and to trust people, and that was okay. It broke Frederic's heart a little every time Sam was afraid or hesitant, though. "Why don't we go," he said instead of trying to comfort Sam. He wasn't sure Sam would accept it.

Sam nodded. "Thank you."

It didn't take long for Frederic to close the door and follow Sam outside. Now that they were there and walking toward Camden's house, Frederic did notice more people looking and staring. He wished they wouldn't, but he understood why they did. Sam wasn't just a novelty because he was a new pack member and a unicorn shifter. Most pack members wouldn't care about either of those things. They *would* care about the fact that he was Frederic's mate. *That* was why they were staring. Everyone cared for Frederic. Their pack was small, so they were more like a big family, and they all wanted Frederic to be happy, and the fact that he'd never brought home a boyfriend made Sam even more incredible to them.

"I hate this," Sam muttered.

"They're not doing it to be mean. They're just curious about you."

"Because I'm a unicorn."

"In part, yes, but mostly it's because you're my mate."

"How can they know that?"

"Well, there aren't a lot of us, and some of us are related. I told my parents and my sister, and I guess they told their friends and our family members. I'm sorry it's making you uncomfortable." Frederic should have asked first, but he'd been so happy to tell his parents about Sam that he hadn't thought about it.

"It's okay. I didn't expect you to keep it a secret. I would have told my parents right away if they'd still been alive."

"I'm sorry for what happened to them." Frederic wasn't a hundred percent sure what had happened yet, but he'd find out eventually. He knew they were dead, though, and that Sam's brother was gone.

"It's been a while."

"Doesn't mean it doesn't still hurt."

Sam finally smiled. "You're right, it does, but I think it's partly my fault. I stayed in the forest on my own for so long. I didn't have anything else to focus on, other people, you know?"

"I understand."

"I'm not sure you do, but then, I'm not sure anyone else can. My life hasn't been like yours, Frederic. Even when I still had my family, it was just us. I don't know how to be with other people. I don't know how to be with *you*."

Frederic's heart broke all over again. "You don't have to know. You'll learn. Besides, it's not like I have that much experience in relationships, and you're different anyway. You're my mate."

"But you have more experience than me. And even if we don't consider the relationship angle, you grew up with a pack. You have friends. You know how to relate to them, how to live a normal life. My life has been anything but normal since I was born, and nothing I can do will change that."

Frederic caught Sam's hand and squeezed it. He started to let go, but Sam tightened his fingers around Frederic's in a silent demand. Frederic was more than happy to obey it and hold his mate's hand. "I know your life hasn't been easy, and that you might always be a bit prickly and unable to relate to people, but that's okay. No one expects you to change much, Sam. Just be you, and you'll manage. I don't need anything else from you." And Frederic hoped it would be enough.

Sam's palms were sweaty by the time he and Frederic arrived at the alpha's house. Sam already knew which one it was. Sage had pointed it out to him, since his was one of the two closest houses. The other one belonged to the pack's beta.

Alpha Cook's house faced the fire pit in the center of the tiny village that was made up by the houses of the pack members. Nothing hindered his few of it, even though it was slightly set back. Sam wouldn't have thought possible for a house to be at the same time the center of the place and private enough, but he had to admit whoever had built this house had done a good job.

"Ready?" Frederic asked. He hadn't said anything about Sam's palm being damp even though they were still holding hands.

Sam swallowed. He wasn't sure he'd ever been less ready for anything, but he didn't have a choice. He could come back later, or another day, but that wouldn't change anything. He had to do this, so he might as well get it out of the way. "Yes."

Frederic smiled encouragingly and knocked on the door. They didn't have to wait long for it to open. A tall man looked down at Sam, then at Frederic. "I already told you, you didn't have to knock."

Frederic smiled. "And I already told you that I'm not going to do that because I've never lived here, and we're not related."

"We've been friends since you were old enough to start following me around."

Frederic scowled. "You don't have to remind me of that every time this argument comes up. And you weren't the alpha back then."

"Maybe not, but you spent as many afternoons here as I did at your parents' place."

The banter between them made Sam think about Toby. His heart ached for his brother. Was he ever going to get him back?

Frederic cleared his throat. "Anyway, this is Sam, my mate."

Sam licked his lips and looked up at the alpha. He hadn't realized Alpha Cook and Frederic were so close when Frederic had talked about him, but now that he did, he couldn't help but wonder what the alpha would think of his childhood friend having him as a mate.

But the alpha just smiled at him and stepped aside. "Come in. And, Frederic, straight to the kitchen. We don't need to go to my office to do this."

Sam looked at Frederic, trying to understand what that meant. *It had to be a good thing, right?* Since Frederic and the alpha were so close and everything. It looked like the alpha was treating Frederic as family, and Sam hoped that meant that would be extended to him—and to his brother.

The house, and especially, the kitchen, smelled of sugar and chocolate. It made Sam's stomach growl, and he looked around, hoping no one had heard it. The alpha was staring right at him, though. He beamed and gestured toward the kitchen table. "Sit down. I'll get you cookies. Do you want milk to go with them?"

"You don't have to do that."

Frederic chuckled and guided Sam toward one of the

chairs. "Don't waste your breath. He'll stuff you full of cookies whether you like it or not."

Sam went along with it. Frederic knew the alpha better than he did, so he knew how to behave.

They didn't talk again until the three of them were at the table. Frederic and Sam both had cookies and milk in front of them, and Sam cautiously took one. He bit into it and groaned because dammit, the last time he'd eaten homemade cookies had been when his mom had still been alive, and these were just as good and brought up memories.

"Good?" the alpha asked.

"Yes, Alpha Cook. Thank you," Sam said after washing down the cookie with some milk.

"Call me Camden. I've never cared about this alpha thing. I mean, when outsiders address me, sure, but you're not an outsider."

Sam swallowed. "But I am. I got here yesterday."

"I'm aware of that. But you're Frederic's mate, and even if you two can't make things work or don't want to, nothing will change that. You're part of the pack now."

Was it really that easy? Sam was about to find out. "Does that extend to my family?"

Camden's smile fell. "Frederic hinted at what happened, but he didn't give me details. And of course, it extends to them. I know your parents are deceased, right?"

Sam didn't want to talk about this. He didn't even want to think about it. But he had to, because of Toby. "It was three years ago, more or less. I didn't even realize so much time had passed until Sage told me what year it is now."

Frederic touched Sam's hand under the table, and Sam grabbed him. He'd never had support, not of this kind, but it would help. It had to.

"We were always loners. My parents knew what would happen if people found out about us."

"Because you're a unicorn," Camden said.

"Yes. Well, because of that story that our horns have healing proprieties."

Sam looked at Camden. He expected him to ask if it was true, then maybe to ask him to help with some healing, but Camden surprised him.

He smiled. "I'm not going to ask you if it's true. I'm not going to use you. If it *is* the truth and you have some kind of healing power, you're the only one who can decide how and when to use it, or even if you want to use it at all. So please, go on."

Was Sam ever not going to be surprised by this pack? If their alpha was anything to go by, the answer was no, and he needed to get used to it.

"So we've always stuck to our little house in the woods. It was lonely sometimes, and it wasn't easy as a teenager, but we made do. Then about three years ago, one night, we were attacked. Men broke into our home. They took my brother and killed my parents because they were trying to keep us safe." Sam closed his eyes. "They somehow forced them to shift so they could cut their horns. I managed to escape, and I wanted to go back, but I knew I'd end up dead like them. I thought the men had killed my brother, too, until I went back the following morning. My . . . parents were there, but Toby was gone." He opened his eyes and looked at Camden. "I haven't seen him since then. I've wanted to look for him ever since, but I was afraid to leave the forest. I've been there since then."

Camden hummed as he thought. "I see. Well, there was gossip about unicorns living in the forest. I wish your parents had reached out to us, but I understand why they didn't think it was a good idea. They didn't know they could trust us. I hope you do, though."

Sam wasn't sure of that, but he nodded anyway. "I'm

starting to understand that."

"Good, because you can. And now that I know about your brother, I'm going to do what I can to find him. I can't promise I'll be able to, or that it's going to be a quick process, but I'll start calling around today. I know this isn't easy for you, but can you tell me everything you remember about the men who killed your parents? How many there were, if they spoke with particular accents, what they looked like? Maybe even names if you can? It would help me identify and locate them."

Sam had thought about what had happened so many times over the years. He knew what he remembered. "I'll write it down. Everything."

Camden smiled. "Good. You can come around any time you want, of course. I'll call you as soon as I find out anything."

"I don't have a phone."

Camden wrinkled his nose. "We're going to do something about that. I know you might not like it, but we have pack funds for this kind of situation. We can buy you clothes, toiletries, and everything you need. You don't have to repay us, but you can once you find a job."

Sam didn't know if he could find a job. His mom had homeschooled him, and he was good at wood working and doing repairs, but was that something he could make a job out of? Or should he use his healing power and help the pack instead? He still wasn't totally sure he could trust them, but he was going to have to make a decision, and soon.

Sam was more relaxed when they left Camden's house, or at least Frederic thought so. Talking about his family and what had happened to them couldn't have been easy, especially not with people he barely knew, but Sam looked better, like maybe he had more faith in the future now. Frederic wanted to reassure him, to tell him he'd find his brother if Camden couldn't, but he knew better than to make promises he couldn't keep. He wanted to find Tobias, but Camden knew people who knew people, so he'd no doubt have better results than Frederic. No, the only thing Frederic could do for Sam was to be by his side and comfort him when he needed it. "Should I walk you home?" he asked. He wanted to spend more time with Sam, but he would understand if Sam needed time to himself. He'd spent his entire life almost on his own. He was used to silence and loneliness.

"Do you think we can, I don't know, walk around? Maybe in the forest?"

Frederic was surprised, but he hoped it didn't show on his face. "Of course. Do you want to shift and go for a run?"

"Not really. I've spent a lot of time as a unicorn, and I'd rather talk to you. Unless you need a run?"

"I don't. I might not have spent as much time as you in my wolf form, but I've been looking for you for a few days. I miss my comfortable life when I'm a wolf."

That got a smile out of Sam, and Frederic felt like he was ten feet tall for managing it. Sam was always beautiful, but especially so when he smiled, because as far as Frederic had seen until now, he didn't do it often.

"You wouldn't have lasted a week in the forest," Sam said, knocking their shoulders together.

"Hell, no. I like air conditioning, heat, my couch, and my TV, and everything else I've worked hard for."

"And that's okay. I guess I like all those things, too. I didn't exactly have a choice. Well, I guess I did, but I didn't know I had one. I couldn't be sure the pack didn't have something to do with what happened to my family."

"I'm sorry you had to go through all that." Frederic hated

to think that he'd been so close yet he hadn't known his mate was there and in pain. He wished he could go back in time, but then if he were able to, he'd try to save Sam's family, no matter the consequences.

They avoided talking about families and the past as they circled the area where the pack's houses were. It was nice to spend some time not thinking about stupid problems and to watch Sam relax even further. It would take him a while to let go of all the wariness in his soul, but Frederic was confident he would, one day. Sam was there to stay, Frederic was sure of that.

He kicked a pebble. He didn't mind the quiet—his family had never been quiet, or at least, his mom and his sister weren't. His dad didn't talk much, but Frederic sometimes wondered if it was because there was already enough noise in the house. Frederic himself wasn't innocent. He'd gone through a phase where he wanted to be a singer, and it had taken him a while to realize his dog at the time howled better than he sang.

Still, he had so many questions to ask Sam. He didn't want to ask about his past because he knew how painful that was for him, so even though he was curious, he kept his mouth shut about that. There were other things to talk about, though. "What do you want to do? As a job, I mean? Not that you have to decide now, but I'm curious to know if you're particularly interested in something."

Sam shrugged. "I don't know. I'm good at fixing things, but I doubt the pack needs someone like that. You probably already have someone."

Frederic grinned. "Yeah, we do. My dad and I."

"You?"

"Yep. What can I say, I'm good with my hands." The second meaning of what Frederic had said went right over Sam's head, and Frederic found it adorable.

"So that's out for me," Sam said. He sounded both relieved and unhappy, which was a weird combination.

"Not exactly. There's more than enough work for you to do it with us. We take care of the entire pack, and sometimes, especially during the winter, we have to hire temporary help. Having you with us would help, and I'd love to work with you, but only if that's what you really want to do. Don't agree to this just because it's what you know. If there's anything else you think you might want to try, you can do it."

"I need to earn my keep, though."

"Don't take this wrong, but the pack and I can afford to give you time to think about your options. I mean, I know you're living with Sage, and that's fine, and I understand why you might not want to accept my money, but I'd be glad to help you, with that or anything else. I don't want you to end up unhappy in ten years because you didn't take the time to think about what you want to do because you felt the need to start working right away." Frederic hoped Sam wasn't going to be offended. He wouldn't be if things were the other way around, but that was just him. He knew some people couldn't stand what they thought of as charity.

"I know people will think I'm supposed to go into healing," Sam said, ignoring what Frederic had just said.

"You shouldn't listen to what anyone says, not even me. Do what you think is right."

Sam smiled. "I think I might want that. I've never done much with my power. I never had to. When I was a kid, and I fell and hurt myself, my parents took care of me. If I do decide that's what I want to do, I'm going to have to learn, though."

"I don't think that's a problem. We have a healer here. She's a wolf shifter, but she can teach you the basics."

They'd walked around the houses as they talked, and

now they were back by Sage's house. They stopped in front of the door, and Frederic hesitated. He wanted to kiss Sam goodbye, but would Sam want that, too?

"Thank you," Sam said.

"I didn't do anything."

"You did more than you think. You're giving me a future I never thought I'd have. You're giving me the chance to choose what I want to be, *who* I want to be. No one else has done that for me."

Frederic rubbed the back of his neck. "I'm just doing what's right."

Sam smiled. "And not everyone would have done that. Just accept the compliment, will you?"

Frederic smiled back. "All right. Will I see you tomorrow?"

Sam looked at the house, then back at Frederic. "Do you want to stay?"

Frederic blinked. "For dinner?"

Sam licked his lips. "For the night. I know it's a bit out of nowhere and that we haven't had the chance to talk, but I'd like you to stay. I . . . well, I think I'd like us to spend the night in the same bed. I don't know what I'm ready for, and the thought of having sex terrifies me, but I don't want you to go, and I realize we'll have to have sex sooner or later."

Frederic's heart felt like it was about to explode. Was it possible that he already loved Sam? "We won't do anything you don't want to do, ever. That means that if you never want to have sex with me, then we'll never do it. I don't care about that, Sam. I only care about you and making you comfortable."

Sam frowned. "But mates have sex."

"I'm sure most of them do, yes. But it's their business, just like what we do is ours. I'll be happy if you only want to make out for the rest of our lives."

Sam looked at Frederic. "Make out?"

"You know, kiss."

Sam rolled his eyes. "I know what making out means, Frederic. I might have lived in the woods for three years, but I didn't *always* live there. I had a house, and a TV."

"Right, sorry. I just didn't want to assume."

"And that's one of the things I like about you. And I want you to kiss me right now. It'll be my first kiss, you know?"

Well, shit. That was a responsibility that scared Frederic a little, but he supposed they'd have plenty of time to repeat it until they both got perfect at it.

Chapter Four

Sam sighed. He couldn't focus on the TV, but then he'd been alternating between watching it and reading for more than a week. He wasn't used to not having anything to do. Even when he'd lived with his parents, or perhaps especially then, he'd had daily tasks to perform, like finding food and making sure the house was safe for the night. But now he only had to open the fridge to find food, and he already knew he was safe in Sage's house. That left him too much time to think, and he didn't like it, not when he couldn't stop wondering if the alpha had found anything about Toby.

It had only been a week, and Sam had been without his brother for three years, but it felt urgent for him to find out what had happened to Toby, what he was doing and if he was safe. Sam wanted to believe he was, but he knew better. The reason he'd been taken wasn't harmless, and he could only hope his healing was what had interested the men who'd taken him. He couldn't even think about what Toby might have been through in the past three years.

So no, Sam didn't want to think about Toby, not yet. He didn't have news, and he didn't want to obsess over it, not when there was nothing he could do.

He tugged his feet under himself and stared at the TV. He wasn't sure what he was watching. He'd put on a movie without even reading the blurb. He just wanted some background noise because the quiet would drive him crazy. Sage was as quiet as a mouse, and Sam didn't know if he was home or not most of the time. He didn't want to bother him, though, just like he didn't want to bother Frederic. He knew Frederic would drop everything and come if he called him, but he didn't want to be needy.

Sam was used to being on his own, so it didn't bother him. What did bother him were the thoughts that churned in his mind because they tended to focus on his brother now that there was a chance to find him, albeit a thin one.

Sam hugged his knees. Maybe he could read. He'd tried that, though, and his thoughts always wandered. He had so much to think about—his brother, his place in the pack, his future, Frederic.

Gosh, Frederic. Sam wasn't sure when it had happened, but he was already falling in love with him. He didn't know what he'd done to deserve a man like his mate, but he was glad he had him. Frederic was quickly becoming one of the few things Sam knew he'd always be able to count on in his life, just like Sage, but in Frederic's case, it was different. He and Sam were mates, and Sam was more tempted to bond with him with every day that passed.

Frederic was giving him the time he needed to get used to this new life, but he was always there, making sure Sam had everything he needed and that he was okay. Sam still wasn't sure what he thought of letting Frederic pay for him until he decided what he wanted to do, but he understood where that proposal had come from, and he was grateful for it. The only two people who'd ever been ready to do that for him had been his parents, and Sam thought it showed how much Frederic cared.

"You've been staring at the wall for the past ten minutes," Sage said as he walked in.

Sam shook himself. "How would you know?"

"I checked in when I went to the kitchen to grab some water." Sage settled on the couch next to Sam. "What are you thinking about?"

Sam sighed and leaned his chin on his knees. "That I wish I could do more, but I don't know what that more is. I'm not used to just hanging around the house. Even when I lived with my parents, there was always something to do, you know? Get wood, make sure the pantry was stocked, things like that. But everything's easy here, and I don't have to worry about any of that."

"That's kind of the point, though, isn't it? Camden wants it so you don't have to worry about those things so you can make the decisions about what you want from life without constraints."

"I know." It certainly had given Sam time to think, as well as to start trusting the pack and Camden. He knew the alpha could just be lying and waiting for Sam to give him something, but he didn't think that was the case. Of course, he could be wrong. He wasn't exactly the best when it came to reading other people, but he didn't want to live the rest of his life never trusting anyone. He might as well go back to live in the forest if this was the way things went.

Did that mean Sam was ready to share his power with the pack, though? He was pretty sure they wouldn't try to use him for it, but he still couldn't be certain of that. Maybe he could ask Camden if he could study with the healer and wait to tell him about his healing power? Camden no doubt suspected Sam had it, but he probably thought it had to do with his horn like everyone else did. The fact that Sam could heal with his body was a well-kept unicorn secret, and it wasn't revealed to anyone they didn't have absolute trust in—and Sam didn't feel that way about Camden and the pack, not yet.

Sage poked Sam in the arm. "Talk to me. I know we're not friends, but—"

Sam looked at him. "We're not?"

"Well, we haven't known each other for long. I understand it takes most people a while to consider someone else a friend. But, well, I like you. I wouldn't have asked you to stay with me in the house otherwise."

"I like you to. And I *do* consider you a friend." If there was one person Sam *knew* he could trust, it was Sage. He wasn't sure why, but he thought it was because they shared something, a vulnerability he didn't share with anyone else. They were both outsiders with the pack, even though Sage had integrated himself perfectly. But Sam hadn't missed the way he spent most of his time in his house rather than out there with the rest of the pack. He knew there had to be a reason, but he hadn't asked. Sage would tell him when and if he felt the time was right.

Sage smiled. "Good. Because I don't care how long we've known each other. You're my friend. And as a friend, I think you should do what you've already decided."

Sam had stopped wondering how Sage always seemed to know so much about what he thought and felt. "And what do think that is?"

"I don't know. I don't actually read thoughts. But I think you know what you want to do with your life, even though you're still hesitant."

"I'd like to be a healer. And it's not because I'm a unicorn."

"Being one is certainly a perk if you choose that kind of work, but it doesn't mean that's what you have to do."

"I know. I just want to be useful." The pack had done a lot for him already, and he wanted a way to thank Camden and everyone else, even though he'd barely spoken to anyone. He saw Sage and Frederic every day, but he'd kept to the house, very much like Sage. Maybe it was time to stop doing that. He wouldn't be able to hide away if he decided to be a healer. Camden had told him he could start working with the pack healer when he wanted, and maybe it was time.

"Go talk to Camden, or Frederic," Sage said. "I know you don't like to rely on anyone but yourself, and I realize it's because you were on your own for so long, but you can trust us." He shrugged. "Although I understand why you might not take my word for it."

Sam startled when his phone rang. He still wasn't used to having one, and he fumbled with it, trying to answer the call. Sage rolled his eyes and took it from him, swiping his finger onto the screen before handing it back.

"Hello?"

"Sam? It's Camden."

"Alpha Cook."

Sam could almost hear the alpha roll his eyes. "I said *Camden*. We'll talk about that when I see you. That's why I called, actually. Do you think you can come around when you have time?"

Sam had only time. "Is now all right?"

"Sure. I baked cookies."

Sam smiled. Camden was a strange alpha, but he seemed like a good man, and not only because Sam had realized how much he still liked homemade cookies.

Frederic wasn't sure what Sam's phone call meant, but he hoped it was that he was starting to trust him. He wanted Frederic with him when he talked to Camden. Frederic wasn't sure about what, but it didn't matter.

They met in front of Camden's house. Frederic arrived first, and he smiled when he saw Sam coming toward him. His shoulders were hunched, shielding himself from the stares, but Frederic noticed that fewer people were looking at him today. The kids certainly weren't, and most their parents and babysitters just smiled and looked away. Sam didn't seem to notice, though. He was too busy ignoring them.

"Hi," Frederic said, greeting him with a smile.

Sam hesitated, then leaned forward. Frederic didn't touch his cheek after Sam had kissed it, but it was a close thing.

He still had a hard time believing this was happening to him. He'd found his mate, and they were working things out. Sam was hesitant, but it had only been a week, and Frederic was confident things would work out. Still, every gesture Sam made toward him made Frederic's heart beat faster.

"Thank you for coming," Sam said.

"Any time you need me, you only need to call."

Sam smiled. "Camden didn't tell me why he wanted to see me."

"I guess we'll find out soon enough. Should I knock?"

"Yes."

Camden scowled at Frederic when he opened, but he didn't say anything about Frederic not just walking in this time. Since it was one of their ongoing private jokes, Frederic knew something was wrong. He hoped Camden's dire expression didn't mean something had happened to Sam's brother, but he was glad Sam had called him, just in case. Frederic couldn't even imagine how Sam would feel if that was the case. He'd already lost so much, and Frederic didn't want him to lose the last member of his family.

"What's going on?" he asked as they followed Camden to his office.

There was a plate of cookies on Camden's desk, so things probably weren't that bad, but still. Camden looked tired and worried. "I'm glad Sam thought about calling you," he said, gesturing at the couch in the corner of his office.

"You have bad news," Sam said. It wasn't a question, as if he knew.

"Not exactly, no. I don't have the best news, though.

Come on, sit down and have a cookie."

"I'd rather go straight to the reason I'm here."

That made Camden smile. "Of course you would. All right." He sat into one of the armchairs. "Okay, so I did some research and asking around like I told you I would. It wasn't easy, not even with the details you could remember from the men who broke into your house and killed your parents, but I did manage to find something." He shuffled in his seat and took out a folded note from his pocket. He held it out to Sam, who took it with a trembling hand.

Frederic hoped Sam wouldn't mind it if he tried to offer him some comfort. Wasn't that why he was there after all? He didn't take Sam's other hand since he was already unfolding the paper, but he reached out and touched his knee, silently telling him he was there and that he wasn't going anywhere.

"Are these the names of the men who killed my parents?" Sam asked.

"Well, I can't know for sure who was specifically responsible—"

"All of them were. They knew why they were in my house. Even if they didn't wield the knives themselves, they're responsible, and I want them to pay."

Camden nodded. "I'll make sure they do. And yes, I think these are the men responsible for what happened to your family. I took your descriptions and sent someone to ask about them in town. It's been a while, though, so I'm not a hundred percent sure of anything, but all the men on this list stayed in the same motel. They arrived the same day and left the same day, and from what Griffin found out, they left in a hurry, and there was someone new with them. The woman who noticed them that day couldn't give us a description of the person they took away, but I don't believe in coincidences, not when they're this big."

Sam clutched the piece of paper like a lifeline. "It was Toby."

"That's what I suspect. We're running the names in all the systems we have access to, and I reached out to some of my friends, but we're a small pack, so we don't have as many resources as I'd like. Griffin went to talk to one of the alphas in the nearest city. I'm hoping that since most of the men on that list seem to still be living there, your brother will be with them."

"Most of them?" Sam dropped his hands to his thighs, He was still clutching the note in one of them, and he grabbed Frederic's hand with the other. He squeezed so hard it hurt, but Frederic didn't protest.

"Some of them are dead, and a few are in jail." Camden leaned forward. "I need to ask you what you want to do, Sam. We're actively looking for Tobias, but it's hard, complicated, and it's going to be a lengthy process. We could try to shorten it, though."

Frederic didn't like this. Camden's expression and his tone were enough for him to know this wasn't going to be good. He shuffled closer to Sam and kept his mouth shut. Whatever Camden had in mind, whatever he asked of Sam, Sam was the only one who could make that decision. Whatever he chose to do, Frederic would support him, even if he didn't like it.

And he was pretty sure he wouldn't.

"The people on that list are well-known hunters," Camden said, nodding at the list. "They capture and sell unique shifters like you and your brother. Unicorns, phoenix, those kinds of beings. They'd jump on the possibility of getting another unicorn."

Fuck. Frederic knew where Camden was going. "You want to use Sam as bait."

Camden nodded. "I know it's not a great idea, and I wish

we didn't need it, but going separately after all of these men would take us weeks, if not months. This way, they'll come to us. We can capture the ones who are involved in this, and Sam can identify them. Then we can ask them where Toby is."

"You think they'll tell us?" Sam asked, his voice too calm and steady. Frederic felt like he was about to explode out of his skin because of the worry and fear crawling there. How could Sam not feel the same way?

"I don't know. Us, maybe not. Like I said, the pack is small, and we're not used to interrogating people. But I also told you I have friends, and some of them are in packs that are much bigger than ours. Some of them live in the city, and they're used to dealing with justice and shifter hunters. I'm sure they'll gladly help as long as we let them punish the hunters the way they think is right."

"That's fine with me. They can all die. I don't care." Sam's voice was harsh, and Frederic's heart hurt for him. He didn't blame Sam for thinking the way he did. Those people had hurt him. They'd killed his parents, had taken his brother, and had left him alone in the world. And if what Camden was saying was true—and Frederic trusted Camden to know what he was saying—Sam's family wasn't the only one they'd destroyed. Frederic couldn't bring himself to feel pity for what awaited them in the future.

Camden cleared his throat. "Good. And Frederic was right. I think we should use you as bait. You'll never be in danger, of course. I'll make sure you're guarded, and the fact that you don't often leave Sage's house will help. Besides, the pack will notice anyone who doesn't belong right away. There are some perks of living in a small pack."

"How are we going to do this?" Frederic asked. He had to know the details because he wasn't going to let Sam out of his sight until those men were behind bars.

"We'll get the word out that a unicorn shifter is living with us. You know how people are with gossip. Word will reach the city in no time, especially if we talk to the right people. Then we'll wait."

Frederic didn't like *that* part of the plan, but it was unavoidable. Hopefully, the hunters would come, and the pack would get rid of them and get Sam's brother back.

Frederic wasn't even going to think about all the ways this could go wrong.

Sam rubbed his face. Gosh, he needed this to be over. It had been three years. Three years of fear and pain, of worry and wondering what had happened to Toby. Sam had never been able to deal with his disappearance, not the way he'd done with his parents. He'd mourned them, had accepted that they were gone. He couldn't do the same for Toby, though.

He didn't even know if his brother was still alive, but he had to believe. He had to believe that they'd find Toby and that they'd bring him home.

And Sam wanted him to have a home. He had no way of knowing what Toby had been through in the past three years, but he could too easily imagine. Toby was going to need a home, a family, and a lot of support. A pack's support.

That meant Sam had to get over his distrust of Camden and his pack and truly become a member. He'd been thinking about it a lot since he'd arrived. He'd watched the pack members from Sage's window. He'd learned which children belonged to who, who was related to who. He'd seen Frederic's family—his parents, his sister and her mate, their child. He trusted Sage.

And there was Frederic. They were mates, and that meant

something. Sam could only go from what he'd seen between his parents, but they'd loved each other. They'd been happy, and he wanted that happiness. He wanted a family, a place where he could feel safe and spend the rest of his life not having to look over his shoulder for people hunting him. He wanted Toby to have all of that, too.

He cleared his throat. "I have to tell you something."

That got Camden and Frederic's attention. They'd been discussing the best way to get the word out that Sam was with the pack, but they stopped as soon as he talked.

Camden looked slightly wary, but Frederic just smiled and squeezed Sam's hand. "Whatever you need."

Again, what had Sam done to deserve such a man? He didn't know, and he didn't care much, either, as long as Frederic remained his. There was one way to be sure of that, but Sam couldn't think of it right now.

He cleared his throat. "About my power. My healing power."

He looked at Camden. He knew Frederic would accept whatever he had to say, but the alpha was an unknown entity. Even though he'd promised Sam he'd be safe, there was still a hint of hesitation in him. He had to get over it, though, if he wanted to make the pack his home and his family.

Camden smiled encouragingly. He didn't say anything, but he didn't have to.

Frederic knew Sam needed to do this of his own volition.

Sam licked his lips. "Everyone thinks the healing powers of a unicorn shifter resides in their horn. That's why the men who took my brother killed my parents and removed their horns." He looked down at where his hand was entwined with Frederic's. "But that's not true. I don't know why people believe that, but that doesn't matter. What *does* matter is that the healing power is real and that every unicorn shifter can use it through their hands. *We* are the healers, not our horns."

Sam had said it. It was the first time he told anyone. His parents had been clear and had repeated it to him since he was a kid—never tell anyone they can use you to heal. Never give anyone the kind of power that knowing the truth would give them over you.

And he just had. He hoped he'd made the right decision, both for himself and for Toby. Because if they managed to bring Toby home, the pack would have two unicorn shifters and twice the problems that came with them.

"So you don't have to be in your unicorn form?" Camden asked.

"No. I use my hands. Well, I've never had the opportunity to do it. There wasn't much need for healing when I was alone in the forest."

"What about when you hurt yourself?"

There went another of Sam's secrets. "My body heals itself quickly. *Very* quickly. I don't need healing unless the wound is particularly bad."

"That's . . . good to know, I guess. And I'm glad you felt comfortable enough with me to tell me, Sam. Thank you."

Sam smiled at Camden. He wasn't sure what he'd expected from the alpha. He remembered some of the shows he'd watched when he was a kid, and there were always gasps and highly emotional reactions when someone came out as anything. Obviously, the TV had gotten that wrong.

"Is there anything else?" Camden asked.

Sam blinked. "Aren't you going to tell me I need to start working as a healer?"

Camden cocked his head. "Didn't I tell you this when you got here? I'm not going to force you to do anything. No one here will. Now, if you actually *want* to work as a healer, I'd welcome it, of course, but I'm not going to ask you to. You're part of our family now. You can stay, whatever you decide to do."

Sam relaxed. He'd known that was the answer he'd get, but a part of him had still doubted. That was gone now. "I do want to become a healer. I've never had the chance to use my power, and I know I could do some good with it. I want that. I just don't know where to start. I've never had any training or anything."

Camden leaned back. "Well, no doubt, the first step would be to have you work and learn with our healer. She's a wolf shifter, so she probably won't be able to help you when it comes to your healing power, but I think it's worth a try. Besides, she can teach you other things, like the power of plants and whatnot. She's been taking care of the pack for years now. I'm sure she has friends who can help you with your . . . quirk, but in the meantime, you can start working."

Sam pressed his lips together to repress a smile. Camden was calling his healing power—a power people were ready to kill to obtain—a quirk? If Sam hadn't already known he was safe with the pack, he would now. Camden had no intention of forcing him to do anything or to taking advantage of him. He wanted Sam to be happy and to do what he wanted with his life, and Sam knew he'd never get an opportunity like this again. "Thank you."

Camden rubbed his forehead. "I'm sure Frederic can take you to Naila. I'd walk with you, but I have a headache, and I want to contact Griffin and the people who are gathering info again."

Sam swallowed. What he was about to do was probably stupid, and there was a high chance he'd fail, but why did he have the power to heal if he wasn't going to use it?

He got up and leaned closer to Camden, ignoring his surprised expression. He touched his fingers to Camden's forehead and closed his eyes.

He knew from watching his mother do it that it should be

as natural as breathing. It wasn't, but he wasn't surprised. Still, he knew the basics, and he used his mind and the touch of his fingers to search for the pain. It took him a moment, but he located it, red and pulsating, right between Camden's eyes. Camden had to be hurting quite badly, yet he hadn't given any hint of it when they'd talked. He was probably used to dealing with those headaches, and while Sam couldn't perform miracles, he *could* help.

He reached out with his power and soothed the pain away. It was harder to do than he'd expected, because the pain was so used to being there. It was deeply seated in Camden, and Sam made a mental note to have him go to the healer to get himself checked. It was probably nothing more than stress, but Sam wanted to be sure.

"That's incredible," Camden breathed out when Sam lowered his hand.

Sam opened his eyes. "I just wanted to do something nice."

"Well, it was. I've been dragging that headache along for two days."

Sam frowned. "You need to see the healer."

Camden touched his forehead with something that looked like awe. "I know, and I will, as soon as your brother is safe. In the meantime, you should probably go meet her. It looks like you have a knack for healing, and we're lucky you want to stay here and help us."

Sam had nothing to say to that. *He* was the lucky one. He'd been alone and homeless, and now he had a family and a home.

Then he realized he didn't know how Frederic had taken his confession. He hadn't said anything about it, and while that might be because he'd been giving a chance to Sam to talk, Sam needed to be sure.

"Do you think she'll be okay with taking me on as her apprentice?"

Frederic smiled at Sam. He could tell Sam was worried, and he didn't like it, but he understood. Sam was still new with the pack, no matter how hard he was trying to fit in. "Of course she will. She's been hounding Camden for years to get an apprentice."

"Why didn't he let her have one?"

"It's not that he didn't let her. It's just that not a lot of people want to become a healer. I doubt it's an easy job, even with your healing power. You'll still have to deal with sick people, with death." Frederic wanted to shield his mate from that. He'd already lost enough in his life. He wasn't the one making decisions, though, not in this case. Sam was free to do what he wanted with his life, and Frederic was humbled that he seemed to want to be with him.

Sam grimaced. "I know. But I like to think there's a reason I'm a unicorn shifter. Not all of us become healers, but maybe if more of us did, we wouldn't be hunted the way we are."

"I doubt it's that easy."

"I know. But the pack has welcomed me even when they didn't have to. I want to thank them, and this is the best way. Besides, I *want* to do this. I've had enough time to think about what I'd do if I ever had the chance to have a normal life. The first thing was finding Toby if I could. The second was helping people. Maybe if my parents had reached out instead of hiding away, they'd still be alive. Maybe if I'd known what to do when they were killed, I would have been able to save them."

From what Frederic knew about what had happened, he doubted that, but Sam's guilt was natural. He pulled on Sam's hand to make him stop walking and wrapped his arms around him. Sam made a little strangled sound, as if he couldn't quite believe Frederic was hugging him, but then he hugged back, sinking against Frederic's body.

Frederic took a risk and kissed the top of Sam's head. "I know you know this, but I'm going to say it anyway. I don't think you would have been able to help your parents, even if you'd been the best healer in the world. The men who killed them knew what they were doing. You'd have been hurt, or worse, killed or taken away. I realize I'm selfish by being glad that didn't happen, but I am."

Sam rubbed his cheek against Frederic's chest, making Frederic's heart go pitter-patter. "Then I'm selfish, too. You don't know how many times I've thought that, only to feel guilty because Toby is who knows where and with whom."

Frederic wanted to promise him they'd find Toby, but he didn't want to lie. "Your brother wouldn't have a chance to be found if you weren't free and with us now."

Sam tilted his face up to look at Frederic. "I know. Some days I wake up in my bed at Sage's house in awe because I'm not dreaming all of this. The pack, the job as a healer, the possibility of finding Toby, and you."

There went Frederic's heart. "Me?"

"Yes. I'm grateful for having found you."

Frederic swallowed. "I know we haven't talked about it, and that the fact that you want to work with our healer is probably answer enough, but you're staying with the pack, right? Even after you find Toby?"

Sam frowned. "I want to. I hope Toby will want that, too."

"What if he doesn't?" Frederic wouldn't blame either of the brothers for wanting to leave this place. They both had horrible memories here.

Sam sighed. "I don't know. I want to say I'll go with him wherever he wants, but it's not that easy. Can we not worry about this yet? I know you want to start planning, but I can't give you an answer. What I can do is promise I won't leave or even make a decision without involving you in it, okay? I love my brother, and I want him to be happy, but I want *you* to be happy as well. It's hard to deal with having to make this kind of decision after the only things I had to think of for three years was whether I'd rather eat grass or shift and grab some of the stuff that's still in the pantry at home."

Frederic didn't miss the fact that Sam still talked about his parents' house as home, and that was okay. He'd refused to go back for now, and Frederic hadn't pushed, but he'd be there when Sam was ready. He was pretty sure that between him and his father they could find a way to avoid having the house crumble to the ground, but they needed Sam's authorization first.

"I want to be with you, Frederic."

Frederic blinked. "I know."

Sam shook his head. "I'm not sure you do. I know we've kissed and everything, but that's not what I'm talking about."

Sam was adorable when he blushed, and he always did when they talked about their relationship or any kind of physical contact. Frederic focused on Sam's words rather than on his face, though, because he could tell this was important. "What are you talking about, then?"

"I'm not ready to bond yet, but I think I will be sooner or later. I want to find out what we can be like, together. I want to stay with the pack and grow old with you. I know it might sound stupid, but I watched my parents together as I grew up, and they were so happy and in love. I want that, too, and I want it with you."

Frederic's heart was going to explode. He knew it. There was no way he could take that level of affection, want, need, maybe even love for the man in his arms.

He cleared his throat. "I'm glad. I want that, too."

Sam nodded. "Good." He rose and kissed Frederic's jaw. "Is the healer waiting for us?"

"Camden probably called her to warn her we were coming."

"Pity. We can see each other later, though, right?"

"I'm coming with you, Sam. Unless you'd rather I go home after I introduce you?"

Sam visibly relaxed. "I'd like you to stay. Please."

"You never have to ask." Fredric kissed Sam's forehead, and they finally pulled apart. He didn't want to, but Sam had things to do and a future to face head-on, and he seemed ready to do just that. Frederic wasn't sure what it would mean for him and their relationship, but Sam wasn't wrong. It was useless to worry now. They weren't even sure they'd be able to find Tobias yet, let alone get him back and bring him home.

Naila was waiting for them in her front yard when they got to her house. She lived deeper in the forest than the rest of the pack but close enough that she could go to anyone's house easily if she was needed. She was standing in the small patch of yard where she grew medicinal herbs, and her eyes glinted when she noticed them.

"You're Sam?" she asked not even looking at Frederic.

Sam hesitated. "Yes. You're Naila?"

"Damn right I am."

Sam leaned closer to Frederic. "I thought she'd be older," he whispered.

Of course, Naila heard him. "You probably also thought I needed a cane to walk around. Get your ass here, Sam. We'll start your lessons right away."

Frederic almost laughed at Sam's shocked expression. Naila was a no-nonsense woman. She had to be to deal with the entire pack. The fact that she was six feet one also helped her keep up her intimidating behavior, but Frederic knew her. She wouldn't hurt a fly.

"That's rosemary," she said, pointing at a small bush. Her jet-black braid hung over her shoulder, and she pushed it back when she crouched next to the plant. "It's used to alleviate muscle pain and boost the immune and circulatory system."

Sam cautiously walked toward her. Frederic wasn't sure what to do, so he hung back, earning himself a smile from Naila.

"Are you going to teach me how to harvest and use those herbs?" Sam asked once he was next to her.

"Of course I am. What kind of mentor would I be otherwise?"

"I'm a unicorn shifter."

Naila snorted. "That's all well and good, but I doubt you can use that power of yours to heal a cold or a fever."

Sam frowned. "I'm not sure. I haven't been taught much about it. My parents died when I was twenty."

"I'm sorry for your loss, and while I can't teach you about unicorn healing, I *can* help you with the rest. I'll also contact other healers and see if they can spare a unicorn apprentice, or even better if I can get a unicorn healer to come around. But first, you need to learn the basics." She pointed at another plant. "That's basil."

Frederic leaned against the closest tree and crossed his arms over his chest. He was going to be there for a while, but he didn't care. Watching Sam start living was a delight, and he'd do it for the rest of his life if he was allowed.

CHAPTER FIVE

"I need you to go into town for me."

Sam looked up from the book he was reading to find Naila leaning over him. "What?"

She rolled her eyes and handed him a piece of paper. "I need you to go into town and grab me these things."

Sam put his book down and took the note. The list wasn't long and included gauzes and over-the-counter painkillers. Naila could have gone herself to get them, and Sam knew she would have if he hadn't been around. So why was she asking him to do it? He couldn't exactly say no, though. He'd been working with her for a week, and he knew she didn't do anything without a good reason, or without what she thought was a good reason.

"I can ask Frederic," he said. He knew what Naila's answer would be before she opened her mouth.

"I want *you* to go, Sam. I would have asked Frederic or someone else if I didn't care who went."

That was what Sam had suspected. He folded the note and clutched it between his fingers. "Why me?"

Naila sighed and tugged on her braid. "Because you need to get used to going into town. I know you haven't been since you got here. Right?"

Sam nodded curtly. He hadn't been since he'd met Sage, and he hadn't been planning on going, either. He didn't want to go into town. If he could, he'd stay in pack territory for the rest of his life. He was just getting used to it, and going into town sounded like an overwhelming, bad idea.

Naila sat in front of Sam at the table in her small kitchen. "You're hiding. You're *still* hiding."

"I'm not. I walk here from Sage's house every day. I even went to the fire pit last night." And he'd been sweating the entire time. He'd been terrified someone was going to say he didn't belong, or maybe attack him to get his horn. Of course, neither had happened. There had been a few stares, but no one had even tried to talk to him, although that probably was because Frederic had been hovering like a mother hen.

"That's good, but you can't spend the rest of your life hiding in pack territory."

Dammit. Naila saw too much. "I'm not hiding," Sam repeated even though neither of them believed that.

Naila tapped her fingertips on the table. "All right. You're not hiding. That means you don't have a problem going, right? You need to get used to doing this kind of errand, to see where the shops you might need are, those kinds of things. I drew you a small map on the other side of the note, and you can either ask someone to drive you or go on foot. Doesn't matter to me." She looked at the clock on the wall. "But I expect you to be back in an hour, so you better go. We need to get some of that bruise salve ready when you're back."

She didn't wait for Sam to protest again—and they both knew he would have. She got up, grabbed the book he'd been reading, and took it away with her. It was hers, so Sam didn't protest even though he wanted to. She'd no doubt give it back so he could continue learning about the plants she used every day.

He rubbed his forehead and sighed. He was going to have to do this. There was no way around it, and he knew he was being ridiculous. He didn't have *unicorn shifter* written on his forehead. No one in town would know, and no one would probably give him a second glance. He was just another pack shifter, nothing more.

He had to believe that if he didn't want to freak out before he even left Naila's house.

He made it to town by pushing through his anxiety and focusing on the trees along the road and what he'd have to buy. It was like a mantra in his mind—gauzes, painkillers, some milk chocolate. Gauzes, painkillers, some milk chocolate.

It worked. Sam barely realized he'd arrived until he almost slammed against a woman walking her dog. He didn't recognize her, so she wasn't a pack member. He apologized and started walking again, his heart in his throat.

But no one even looked at him. He'd expected the same stares he got in pack territory even though he knew it probably wouldn't happen.

It wasn't happening. Everyone was going on with their day, walking around Sam and ignoring him. This was the most anonymous he'd been since he'd left the forest, and before that, well, he'd been anonymous only because he was alone.

Sam started to relax. He wasn't entirely comfortable as he walked into the stores and bought what Naila needed, but things could have been much worse. He doubted he'd want to come back to town anytime soon, but it wasn't as terrible as he'd expected. Still, he couldn't wait to go back home.

But he knew Naila was right—he wanted to go home because he was more comfortable hiding. He needed to get out of that state of mind, though. If he wanted to be part of Frederic's life and a pack member, he couldn't continue avoiding people.

He stood on the sidewalk and looked at the coffee shop. One of the pack members worked there. Sam could see him through the window, talking and smiling to customers, handing them their drinks. Sam swallowed. He'd never had one of those fancy drinks. He'd tried enough things by now to know he preferred tea to coffee, but it was always Sage or Frederic who prepared them for him. He'd even tried his hand at it. Some of the drinks on the boards above the counter looked good, though, and Sam squinted to read what was in them.

Caramel, vanilla, chocolate, even whipped cream and sprinkles. He could make a dessert out of his coffee if he wanted.

The rumble of several motorcycles made him look away from the shop. There were three of them driving into town, and while the men riding them wore helmets, making it impossible for Sam to see their faces, they made him feel queasy and like he needed to run away.

He walked into the coffee shop. He felt better as soon as the door closed behind him. He looked around, but everyone was busy with their things, and no one said anything as he walked up to the counter and smiled at Jarvis. Jarvis beamed back. "Sam! I didn't expect to see you here. First time?"

Sam nodded. "Yes. It's . . . weird."

"I bet. What's your poison, then? Coffee or tea? It's on me."

"I can pay."

"I know you can, but it's your first time. Come on. Choose something."

There were too many options, so Sam decided to go with something he knew he'd like. "Tea, please."

Jarvis grinned. "That's all you're going to give me? Okay. I can work with that." He disappeared behind the huge machine he used to make coffee.

Sam watched him work. He couldn't have explained half the stuff Jarvis did, but the result was a tea that smelled so good it made Sam's stomach growl.

"It's chai tea," Jarvis told him. "I didn't put a lot of stuff in it since it's your first, just some vanilla, but maybe next time we can try something different?"

"Of course. Thank you."

Jarvis' smile widened. He pointed at a table in the corner. It was partially hidden behind a bookcase, and it was empty. "Go sit there. No one will bother you. Hell, no one will probably notice you. You can drink your tea in peace."

"Thank you." Sam wasn't sure what else to say. He wasn't surprised Jarvis had noticed he liked being on his own, but he hadn't expected Jarvis to make sure he felt comfortable the way he had.

Sam was glad for the hiding place when one of the men on the motorcycles came in. He was holding his helmet, and he went straight to Jarvis, leaning over the counter to talk to him. Jarvis' smile vanished, and he shook his head several times. Then he gestured toward the door, and Sam held his breath. Was the biker going to hurt Jarvis for not giving him what he wanted, whatever that was?

He left, stomping his boots to the door and letting it slam behind him. Jarvis still looked worried, though, and he briefly talked to the other men behind the counter before moving out from behind it and making a beeline for Sam. He slid into the chair opposite him. "He was looking for you."

"What?"

"He asked if I knew anything about a unicorn shifter."

So Camden's plan had worked. The bad guys had come to find Sam, and of course, it was on the one day he wasn't in pack territory. "Thank you."

Jarvis shook his head. "Don't thank me. I didn't do anything. But you should probably leave before the guy comes back. Just try to act normal, okay?"

Sam wasn't sure what acting normal was, but he nodded.

He waited until Jarvis was back behind the counter to text Frederic, then he got up.

It was hard to make his legs move toward the door. He wanted to stay where he was and hide, but he forced himself to move. He pushed the door open and stumbled out, slamming against someone who was coming it. He looked up, an apology on his lips, and froze.

The man who'd been there that night, the man who'd killed his parents, was looking down at him.

"Naila? Sam?" Frederic called out as he got to Naila's house. He was late meeting Sam, and he hadn't even been able to call him because he'd forgotten his phone somewhere.

"I guess I should be happy at least one of you showed up," Naila said as she came out of the kitchen, drying her hands on her apron.

Frederic frowned. "What do you mean? I know I'm late for lunch, but Sam came here this morning. I walked him part of the way."

"I know he did. I sent him into town to do some errands for me."

Shit. "Into town?"

Naila sighed. "He's going to have to learn to leave pack territory sooner or later. You can't keep him hidden here, not when so much of the world is outside."

"I know that, and trust me, I'm not trying to keep him here. But leaving pack territory isn't safe for him."

Naila frowned. "What do you mean?"

"Camden put the word out that there's a unicorn shifter in town to try to draw out the people who have Sam's brother."

Naila's eyes widened. "No one told me about that."

"That's because Camden didn't want it to be known. He

knew the pack would try to protect Sam."

"That's a good thing."

"It is, but we need those people to come here." And knowing Sam's luck, they'd probably chosen that day to get into town. "Dammit. I can't even call Sam because I can't find my phone."

"You left it here last night."

"I did?"

Naila went back to the kitchen, coming out a minute later with Frederic's phone in his hand. The battery was on the red, but it was enough for Frederic to see Sam had texted him today. He opened the text, praying his phone wouldn't choose to die when he most needed it, and read it.

Men looking for me in town. I'm at the coffee shop, but I'm going to try to come home.

Frederic swore. Why hadn't Sam stayed where he was? At least if those men recognized him or realized he was the shifter they were looking for, he'd be safe. There was always a crowd in the coffee shop, and Frederic doubted anyone would try to grab Sam in there. But if Sam had left . . .

"I need to go," he said. He tried to answer Sam's text, but his phone chose that moment to die.

"What's going on?"

"Someone in town is looking for Sam. He texted me."

"Call him." Naila took her phone out of her pocket and handed it to Frederic.

Frederic shook his head. "You call him, and Camden. Tell him everything Sam tells you."

"And if Sam doesn't answer?"

God, Frederic didn't want to think about what that would mean. "Keep on trying once you've talked to Camden. Tell Camden Sam was at the coffee shop and that some guys are in town looking for him. Oh, and that I'm headed to the coffee shop, although I think he'll realize that on his own." Camden would go straight there too if his mate was in danger. Not that he'd met his mate yet, but any decent person would do it, and Camden was more than decent.

Frederic didn't waste time. He dumped his phone into Naila's hand and ran out, toward his house. He wanted to shift and run to town as a wolf, but he didn't want to waste time having to find clothes once he got there. He was glad he'd gone for his car when he noticed Reece hanging around on his porch. Reece looked up, alarmed, and when Frederic gestured at him to climb into the car, he didn't hesitate.

"What's going on?" he asked once Frederic was driving toward town.

"Guys in town asking about Sam. He's there right now. Naila sent him out on errands."

"Shit."

"Pretty much, yeah."

"Do you know where in town he is?"

"He texted me from the coffee shop, but he was leaving."

"Is Jarvis working?"

"I don't know. Hopefully." Maybe he'd been able to stop Sam from leaving if he was there.

Frederic knew he was driving too fast and he didn't care. He barreled onto Main Street and turned into the parking lot closest to the coffee shop, almost running over a lady holding grocery bags. She didn't even flinch because she was too busy staring at something in the back of the lot.

Frederic followed her gaze and swore. "Dammit. He left." At least now Frederic was closer to Sam, though. He just wished he hadn't found him in this kind of situation.

Sam's back was pressed against the wall. He was clutching shopping bags in his hands and looked like he wanted nothing more than to get away from the man leaning over him.

The man was tall. His long hair was tied back, and his forearm was against the wall just above Sam's head, bringing him so close to Sam that he could kiss him if he wanted to. He was big, and Sam wouldn't be able to do much to him, not in his human form. He might be able to in his unicorn form, but Frederic doubted he was going to shift, not in public. Even if he no doubt wanted to skewer the guy with his horn, he wouldn't give him the advantage of knowing who he was facing, not this early.

Frederic jumped out of the car, ignoring Reece's swearing and calling, and ran toward Sam. Sam's gaze shifted to him, and he relaxed, but the guy hovering leaned even closer, until his nose was a breath away from Sam's neck.

Frederic was going to kill the fucker. "What's going on here?" he asked when he got to them.

The man moved back, but he was still too close. "None of your business."

"It is when you're freaking my mate out."

The guy blinked. "Your mate?"

"Yes."

"He didn't tell me he was mated."

"I don't care what he told or didn't tell you. Leave him alone."

The guy finally stepped away. He raised both hands in an attempt to placate Frederic. "Sorry, man. I was just telling him that he reminded me of someone."

"I doubt you know him. He doesn't leave pack territory much." Frederic moved closer and opened his arms. Sam dumped the bags he was still holding and rushed into his arms, burying his face against Frederic's chest. Frederic could feel Sam's heart race when he gently touched his neck, and he rubbed his pulse with his thumb, trying to calm him down.

"Just go," Reece said to the man.

Frederic didn't care about the guy anymore. He held Sam close and murmured things that probably didn't make sense to him until he finally relaxed. Then Frederic looked up to make sure the guy was gone.

Reece stood close by, Jarvis with him. They were talking, and they were both glancing at Sam and Frederic every so often. They were worried, that was plain to see, and Frederic shared that sentiment.

He gently pulled on Sam's hair. "What happened?"

"It was the man. The one who killed my parents."

"It was him?"

Sam nodded, rubbing his cheek against Frederic's chest. Frederic wanted to go after the asshole and tear him to pieces, but Sam was more important than revenge. Frederic rubbed his back. "He's gone now."

"I want to go home, Frederic."

"Of course. I'll take you."

Frederic looked at Reece, who waved at him. "Jarvis is driving me. He's going to tell me more about the guy who asked if he knew Sam." And he and Jarvis would make sure Frederic and Sam wouldn't get ambushed on their way home. Frederic smiled in thanks and steered Sam toward the car.

"Wait. The bags," Sam said.

Frederic snatched them from the ground, mentally cursing at Naila. Did she really have to push Sam today of all days? She couldn't have known, but this was bound to make Sam stick even more to what he knew and where he felt safe, dammit.

Frederic dumped the bags in the back seat and made sure Sam was buckled in before leaving the parking lot. He couldn't help but look around, searching for the guy he wanted to pound into the ground and his friends. He didn't see them anywhere, but he wasn't surprised. Those guys were still around three years after killing Sam's parents. They knew what they were doing. They were professionals.

Which was why he also wasn't surprised when Reece called on Sam's cell almost as soon as he and Sam walked into Frederic's house to tell Frederic they'd been followed.

Sam hated waiting, which was ironic since he'd been waiting for something like this to happen for the past three years. But now that he knew the people who had his brothers were close, he wanted to go after them and get them to tell him where Toby was. Well, himself or Frederic, or even Camden. He wouldn't be picky, and he knew he wasn't intimidating enough to get answers out of anyone.

"How are you feeling?" Frederic asked.

Sam wasn't sure what he'd been doing after he left him on the couch, but he could see he was still worried. He forced himself to smile. "I'm fine. I could have done without having to face the man who killed my parents, but I'm okay. I mean, we're going to get him, right?"

Frederic's smile looked like Sam's had felt—forced and stiff. "I hope so. Camden is coming here, so we can talk about what happens next."

"We'll go after him. We have to."

"I know your first instinct is to do that, but we have to be smart about this, not rash. Things are going to be a mess if we run into this without thinking about it, and I don't want to lose you, Sam."

Sam leaned back against the couch. He knew what Frederic was saying was right, but how was he supposed to sit around when the man who might still have his brother was in town? How could he justify not doing everything he could to get his brother back right now?

"Just wait until Camden gets here, okay? We'll talk to him and see what he wants to do," Frederic begged.

Camden was Sam's alpha now. Sam owed him respect

and obedience, just like he'd owed them to his parents. He just hoped that obeying Camden and waiting for him to come up with a plan wouldn't end up in death like it had for his parents. They'd told him to run that night, to hide and wait for them to come get him.

They never had.

Sam was grateful for the knock on the door that signaled Camden's arrival. He wanted to stop thinking about all this, but it was impossible because it would mean he'd have to stop thinking about Toby, and he didn't think he'd ever be able to do that.

"Hey, Sam," Camden said as he walked in. "Frederic told me you had quite a morning."

"The men who killed my parents are in town."

Camden nodded and sat on the coffee table in front of Sam. "I know you want to go after them. It's only natural. I also know they followed you and Frederic to pack territory, though, so they'll no doubt see you if you leave the house. You should stay here, at least for the night."

"What are you going to do while I stare at the walls?" Sam hated the bitter tone in his voice, but he couldn't do anything about it. He felt bitter, even after everything the pack had done for him. It wasn't enough because Toby was still out there.

But Camden didn't look offended by Sam's less than grateful attitude. "Well, to start, I'm going to find out who exactly the three men who arrived today are. I've already assigned someone to keep an eye on them since they're in pack territory."

"That's illegal."

Camden smiled. "I know that, but I doubt they care about that kind of detail. Whoever they are, they've been hunting shifters for a while."

"And it's an offense punishable by death." Shifters were

generally peaceful—they had to be to live with humans. Their numbers had been rising over the past decades, and a lot of humans didn't like that fact, and they weren't shy about letting it be known. They were afraid, and Sam could understand that. But just like shifters were prohibited from hunting humans, humans were prohibited from hunting shifters. If it happened, the hunted race could take care of justice without asking the other race its opinion. In shifters' cases, the human hunters never lived for long. Camden was going to gather as much proof as he could on those humans—then he was going to kill them.

Sam was okay with that.

He wished he could do something, anything, but he realized he had to step back and be a spectator in this case. It would be better for everyone. Knowing himself, Sam would end up messing things up, and those men would escape. As much as he hated it, his place was right where he was on Frederic's couch.

Camden got up and patted Sam's shoulder. "I know it's hard, but please, trust me. I'm going to do everything I can to save your brother and bring him home. I promise."

Sam believed him. He hoped he was doing the right thing, but he believed him. "Thank you."

"Stay here with Frederic. That way I won't worry that you might get caught or hurt."

"What if they try to come in?"

"Then we'll arrest them. They're not going to hurt anyone else. I won't let them."

Camden and Frederic talked for a moment before Sam heard the front door open and close again. He tried to relax, but he wasn't sure he'd be able to, not with the possibility of finding Toby so close he could taste it.

Frederic came to sit next to Sam once Camden was gone. "Can I do anything? I hate seeing you like this."

Sam's heart swelled. The last time anyone had cared about him this way, it had been his mom and his dad. He'd been so deeply alone the past three years that he'd thought he wouldn't be able to get used to it again, that he wouldn't be able to make himself care for anyone.

He'd been wrong. God, he'd been so wrong. He cared for Frederic, probably more than he should even though they were mates. He wasn't sure if that bond between them was the reason he cared or if it was just Frederic. It would have been so easy to fall in love with Frederic even if they hadn't been mates, though. He'd been taking care of Sam since Sam had arrived in pack territory, but he'd never made Sam feel like he was hovering or pushing too much. He was giving Sam the time he needed to think things out and to start trusting him and the pack.

He was perfect. There was no way Sam could have stopped himself from falling in love with him.

And he was now. There was no denying it, even though he'd never been in love before. Frederic filled all of Sam's thoughts, awake and asleep. Sam wanted to make him happy, to be with him from the moment they both woke up in the morning to the moment they went to bed at night. He wanted to see Frederic's hair grow gray and his face wrinkle and know that no matter how much time passed, their love would never fade.

He was in trouble, and he didn't even care. He *liked* this kind of trouble. He wouldn't have all he had now if he and Frederic hadn't met at the stream. He wouldn't have a home, friends, a job, a lover. He wouldn't have a future.

He opened his mouth to tell Frederic all that, but another knock on the door interrupted him. Frederic held a finger. "Hold that thought. I'll see who's at the door and send them away. Then we can talk about whatever's on your mind."

Sam wasn't surprised Frederic knew he'd been having

important thoughts. He smiled and nodded, and watched Frederic get up and leave the room.

He winced when he heard the voice as soon as Frederic opened. "What's happening?"

Sam knew who it was even though he hadn't yet met Frederic's mother. He'd heard her plenty of times around pack territory, and he'd always made sure she didn't see him. It wasn't like he didn't want to meet her, but he was terrified of it. What if she didn't like him? What if she didn't think he was good enough for her son? Frederic wouldn't let her decide their future, and he'd be with Sam if that was what he wanted—and Sam knew it was—but he'd be sad, and Sam wasn't ready to deal with that.

He also wasn't ready to deal with meeting Frederic's parents, but it looked like that was exactly what was about to happen.

Frederic did *not* want to deal with his mom right now. "Nothing happened?"

She narrowed her eyes. "Bullshit."

Frederic was used to hearing her curse, so he didn't say anything about that. "What do you know?" he asked instead. She always knew everything, but he didn't want to give her info Sam might not want her to know.

"Someone saw you running to your car. Reece got into it with you, and you left, and someone called Camden and put him in a state of emergency."

Did she have spies going around pack territory and reporting to her? "Everyone is fine."

"Then tell me what happened. And let me in, will you? Why am I still standing outside?"

She moved toward Frederic, but he held a hand up. "I'm not asking you to stay outside, but Sam is here."

Her eyes widened. Like everyone in the pack by now, she knew Sam's story. She knew he was a unicorn shifter, that he'd lost his family, and of course that he was Frederic's mate. She'd gotten her info directly from Frederic, but she and Sam hadn't met yet. Sam hadn't met anyone from Frederic's family. Frederic didn't mind. Sam had needed some time to adjust, and he was doing incredibly well. Meeting the family could wait.

Although it looked like it wouldn't.

"Can I make sure he's okay?" Frederic's mom asked.

"He is."

"I know you want to protect him, and I promise I won't say anything bad, but come on, Freddy."

Frederic sighed. "Come in, Mom. But you're not staying. I'm planning to have a nice, relaxing night with my mate." Frederic wasn't sure how much they could relax considering everything that was happening, but they were going to try. He wanted to make Sam forget for a few hours, and hopefully, Camden would have news for them by then.

He stepped aside and let his mom in, closing the door behind her. She smoothed her shirt down. "What do you think?" she asked.

Frederic blinked. "About what?"

"About how I look. I want to make a good first impression."

"Mom, you're not interviewing for a job. Sam won't care about your shirt or what you look like."

Sam was in the living room, standing by the window and looking like he was thinking about sneaking out through it. The thought made Frederic smile. Both his mate and his mom were nervous, but they had no reason to be. He knew they'd love each other. He was just praying his mom wouldn't push too hard, too fast. She'd wanted to pull Sam in the fold ever since she'd found out about him, and sometimes, she was a little much.

"Hello, Sam. I'm Julia, Frederic's mother."

Sam bit his lower lip and forced a smile. "Hello. I'm, well, Sam, but you already know that. You also already know I'm Frederic's mate. I'm . . . not sure what to say at this point, I'm sorry." He looked at Frederic, silently asking for help. Frederic was more than happy to give it to him.

He smiled. "Mom was just making sure we're okay. She heard something happened today, and she was worried."

Sam cocked his head. "About me?" He sounded like he didn't quite believe that.

"Of course about you!" Frederic's mom exclaimed. "And about Frederic, too, but I know he can take care of himself. And now that I've seen both of you are fine, I'll leave you to whatever you were doing. Sam, are you feeling up to coming to dinner on Sunday? I'd like to spend some time to get to know you, but only if you want it too."

Frederic wanted to intervene and tell his mom to back off, but Sam was an adult, and he wasn't as fragile as Frederic imagined him to be. He'd just faced the man who had killed his parents, and he hadn't broken down crying or punched the guy. He could face Frederic's mother. She wasn't going to eat him. If anything, she might kill him with niceness.

Sam looked at Frederic, who nodded in what he hoped was an encouraging manner. Sam bit his lower lip. "All right. Thank you for inviting me, Mrs. Hunter."

"Please, call me Julia."

Frederic loved his mom, but he was glad to see her go. She was best dealt with in small doses, just like the rest of Frederic's family. Well, except his father, but his dad would never have barged into his house the way his mom had. No, he'd have sent his wife—which was probably what had happened now that Frederic thought about it. His dad always found a way to find out everything that happened with the pack. That was why he often worked with Camden even though he wasn't in the pack hierarchy.

"That wasn't so bad, was it?" Frederic asked when he went back to the living room after seeing his mom out.

"She's, well, a mom, I guess."

"That she is, and she's going to try to mother you, too. You need to be clear with her when it comes to that if you don't want it. She won't be offended, but she needs to know."

Sam smiled softly. "I don't know. I missed having a mother. It won't be the same, but maybe it's a step toward having a normal life again."

Could Frederic love Sam more than he already did? He'd expected a rejection, and he would have understood it. Sam had lost his mom in the most horrible way. Frederic didn't know how he'd deal if something like that happened to his parents. The way Sam was coping was impressive.

"What do you want to do for the rest of the day?" Frederic asked.

Sam stared at him without answering. Frederic wondered if he'd said something wrong, tensing when Sam got up and came toward him. He stopped in front of Frederic and looked up at him.

"I think I'm ready."

Frederic frowned. "Ready for what?" He hoped Sam wasn't planning on hunting the asshole who killed his parents.

Sam hesitantly reached for Frederic. He wrapped his arms around Frederic's neck and looked up at him again, but his gaze stopped at Frederic's chin as if he couldn't look him in the eyes. "You know."

Frederic had a pretty good idea of what Sam was saying, but he wanted to be sure. He was terrified of scaring Sam off by doing or saying the wrong thing. He realized he'd have to get over that eventually, but Sam's was already going through so much. Frederic didn't want to be an utter cause of distress. "What are you ready for exactly, Sam?" he asked.

Sam rose and kissed Frederic's jaw. "Take me to your room."

Frederic licked his lips. "Are you sure?"

"Yes. I've been thinking about this, and I've been sure for a while. I just haven't had the right occasion to bring it up."

Frederic thought any occasion was right to being that up, but he was used to sex, so he didn't fully understand what Sam was going through. He was twenty-four and still a virgin. Frederic would never know how that felt.

He stepped away and took Sam's hand. While he wanted Sam to be sure, he wasn't going to keep asking. Sam knew he'd stop if he wanted him to. He just had to say the word.

They fell on Frederic's bed, their legs entwined. Frederic should probably have thought about getting both of them naked before doing that, but it was fun to watch Sam trying to figure out how to get his pants off without moving away from Frederic. He made a frustrated noise and pushed Frederic away. Frederic laughed and stripped without looking at what he was doing. He was watching Sam instead, remembering what his body looked like.

It was different from the first and only time Frederic had seen him naked. He was still pale and long-limbed, still thin and with no muscle definition, but he'd been eating better since he'd moved in with the pack, and it showed. He looked healthy now—his skin golden in the afternoon light. He didn't have any shame in his body as he exposed it and spread himself out on the bed.

Frederic didn't know where to start. He wanted everything with Sam, but he also wanted to take things slow. They'd have the rest of their lives together to do acrobatics in bed. Right now, Frederic wanted something warm and slow and full of love, but he wasn't sure how to ask for it. He wasn't sure what Sam expected from him, but they made it work. Sam didn't seem to be in a hurry, and Frederic was glad. He wanted both of them to enjoy the slow sliding of their bodies together, the smell of sweat and sex in the air, the feeling of the sheets on their skin, tangling with their legs.

Sam had sex the way he did everything—he was hesitant, careful, but once he realized Frederic couldn't care less what he did, he got surer. He didn't ask for anything, but he took what he wanted, touching Frederic, squeezing him, rubbing their bodies together.

That was all they needed for now. There was no lube, no penetration, just the sliding of bodies and the search for pleasure.

And Frederic wouldn't have had it any other way.

Chapter Six

Sam jerked away when the hand landed on his mouth. He didn't think—he wouldn't have been able to even if he'd tried—grabbing the hand and trying to push it away.

It was that night all over again—hands on him, his parents pulling him out of bed and telling him to run, the screams and pleas, the dark laughter. All of that flashed into Sam's mind, and he fought harder. He needed to get free. He needed to run, to save himself.

"It's me," Frederic murmured, catching one of Sam's wrists with his free hand. He pushed it against the pillow.

Sam froze. Why was Frederic making sure he couldn't speak or scream? What was going on?

Frederic waited for Sam to nod to remove his hand. "Sorry I had to do that."

Sam didn't care about that right now. "What's going on?" Because there had to be a reason for Frederic to do this.

They'd fallen asleep naked in each other's arms last night, and while they were still naked from what Sam could see, the mood was definitely different. He doubted Frederic had woken him up for a bout of nightly sex, which was a pity, and not only because it indicated a problem.

"I heard a noise downstairs," Frederic said, leaning close enough that Sam could feel his warm breath against his ear.

Sam couldn't move. He'd only experienced this kind of fear once in his life. Even his meeting with the man who'd killed his parents earlier hadn't scared him as much as Frederic's words had just now. He'd been in town then, with people walking around, so he'd known he was safe, even only relatively. Now, though? The only thing he could think of was coming home to find Frederic's body on the floor like he had when his parents had died.

He gripped Frederic's arm. "You have to stay here."

Frederic shook his head. "I need to go see what's going on. It might be nothing."

"You said you heard a noise. That means it was loud enough to wake you, right?"

"Yes, but I'm a light sleeper."

"I don't care. You can't go." Sam wouldn't be able to stand it if he lost Frederic, too. He'd just gotten used to the thought that he had a family again, a future. He wasn't going to lose everything again.

Frederic cupped both of Sam's cheeks with his hands and forced him to look at him. "I know you're scared."

Sam snorted. "You don't know anything. You don't know what it's like to have your mother tell you to run and hide and to come home to find her and your father dead. How can I let you go downstairs when it could mean I lose you?"

"You won't lose me, Sam. You know Camden had men stay outside the house. That's why it's probably nothing. They would have noticed it if someone had tried entering."

"Then what was the noise you heard? And if no one is there, you don't have a problem if I come with you, right?"

Frederic grimaced, giving Sam all the answers he needed. "Sam—"

"Frederic. You know there's someone downstairs. Call Camden or the people who were supposed to keep an eye on the house. But don't go downstairs alone, please."

Frederic kissed Sam's forehead. "I'll be fine. I promise. I won't do anything stupid. I just want to make sure someone is there before I call Camden and freak out. You, though, have to stay here."

"But—"

"No. You have to stay here because if it *is* the man who killed your parents, he's going to do anything he has to to grab you and I can't focus on keeping myself safe when you're in danger."

"You play dirty."

Frederic grinned, and Sam could see it even in the dark. "I know. Anything to keep you safe."

Sam didn't want to stay in the bedroom, but he understood what Frederic was saying, no matter how little he liked it. He huffed. "Fine."

Frederic nodded. "Good. Get dressed and stay in here. I'll be back soon."

Sam hadn't noticed Frederic was already wearing jeans. He got out of bed and grabbed his clothes from the chair where he'd put them after the first time they'd had sex. By the time he was dressed, Fredric had snuck out of the room.

Sam resisted the urge to go after him. He wanted to, and he thought he could help, but after what Frederic had said about being too worried about him to focus, he didn't want to risk it. He'd never forgive himself if something happened to Frederic because of him.

What the fuck was he supposed to do while he waited, though? He hoped Frederic would be back soon, but he'd been in this situation before, or in a situation that was close enough to this one. He knew waiting was going to make it feel like time was crawling, and he wasn't sure he could stand that.

Sam crept toward the bedroom door. Frederic had left it slightly open, and Sam tried to hear something, anything that would tell him Frederic was okay. The house was silent, though, and it didn't help him feel better. Was there really someone, or had Frederic dreamt the noise he'd heard? And if there *was* someone in the house, why couldn't Sam hear anything? He would if Frederic were fighting the guy, but he couldn't hear a fly.

He licked his lips. His mouth was dry, and he couldn't stand still. He moved away from the door and looked out the window. Everything was as it was supposed to be. The other houses were dark and silent, and no one was around. Sam didn't even know what time it was, but he was ready to bet it was early in the morning. That was when his home had been attacked the first time. Everyone had been asleep, and the men who'd taken Toby had used that to their advantage.

The door creaked open, and Sam turned, a smile on his face. He was ready to tease Frederic about the fact that he'd freaked out for nothing.

But he hadn't.

Because it wasn't Frederic who opened the door. No, it was the man who'd killed Sam's parents.

Sam was frozen in place. He watched the man grin and opened the door even more, then stepping into the bedroom. "I thought I'd recognized you," he said.

Sam wasn't sure he could say anything—that he could get words that made sense out of his mouth. Besides, he didn't want to talk to this man.

He wanted to kill him.

He moved toward him, but the man raised a gun and tsked. "I don't think so, pretty boy."

Sam balled his hands into fists. "You killed my parents."

"Yeah, yeah. I see you're still not over it? Well, I don't care." He waved the gun toward the door. "Come on."

"What do you want from me?"

"I think you know what I want from you."

"Where's my brother?"

The man cocked his head. "Do you want to find out?"

"Of course I do!"

"Why don't you come with me, then? I'm sure the people I sold him to can do with a second unicorn."

Sam's stomach felt like lead. He didn't want to go with this asshole, but what if this was his only chance to find Toby? He couldn't hear anything or anyone else in the house, and while he was worried sick about Frederic, he knew his mate could defend himself. And if something had happened to him . . . no. Sam didn't want to think about that. He *couldn't* think about that. Frederic was fine, and this was Sam's chance to find his brother. Besides, it wasn't like the man with the gun would take no for an answer. Sam could probably try to run away, but the man had a *gun*. What was to say he wouldn't just shoot, force Sam to shift, and cut his horn like he'd done to Sam's parents?

Sam swallowed. "I'll come with you."

The man grinned. "Of course you will if you want to live. You're not as dumb as your parents, obviously."

"Don't talk about my parents that way."

"Why? What will you do to me if I do?" He waved the gun around. "I have all the power here, boy. Now come on. We should leave before your boyfriend comes back."

Sam looked around before following the man out of the room. He hoped he'd be back, and that he'd have Toby with him.

And he prayed Frederic was okay and safe.

Frederic crept around the corner. He needed to get to his phone, and he'd stupidly left it on the kitchen counter to charge. He'd been too focused on Sam, and he'd made a mistake. He hoped Sam wouldn't have to pay for it. He wouldn't be able to forgive himself if he did.

The kitchen was empty, and Frederic moved inside. His phone was right there, but before he could reach the counter, a shadow told him he wasn't alone anymore.

He wasn't a warrior, but that didn't mean he couldn't defend himself. Camden made sure every pack member who wanted to learn to fight could, and that even those who didn't, knew self-defense.

The person—it had to be a man from what Frederic could feel—grabbed Frederic from the back, wrapping his arm around Frederic's throat and squeezing. Frederic knew he'd faint if he didn't do something fast, and he prayed his attacker wasn't holding a gun in his free hand. He didn't think so, though, because if he had, he'd have no doubt threatened Frederic with it. That was what guns were for after all.

Frederic had to risk it.

He stomped one of his feet onto one of the man's shoes, hitting back with his elbow at the same time. It was simple—and effective. The man jerked back, allowing Frederic to turn around and punch him in the stomach. The man folded in half, and Frederic grabbed his head, jerking his knee up at the same time. The crunch of bone was sickening yet oddly satisfying.

Frederic let the man drop to the floor and checked him for a gun. He found one tucked into the man's waistband and took it out, rolling his eyes. He dumped it into the sink and grabbed his phone.

There was a missed call from Camden, and Frederic returned it.

"Freddy, thank God," Camden said when he answered.

"What the fuck, Cam? Where is everyone? You guys were supposed to be around tonight, yet there's a bleeding man in my fucking kitchen," Frederic snapped, making sure to keep his voice low even though it wasn't as satisfying as yelling.

"I know, I know. But someone set fire to Naila's house. Everyone went there when we realized."

"Shit. Is she okay?"

"Yes, and the fire didn't do a lot of damage. We're on our way back. Is the guy on your floor the only person in the house? Because there were at least three of them."

Shit. Fredric needed to check the rest of the house, and he needed to do it now. "I don't know."

"Go. We'll be there in five minutes."

Frederic dropped his phone back on the counter and left the kitchen. He moved slowly even though he was in a hurry to go back upstairs and check on Sam taking his time to check the bathroom by the kitchen, then the living room.

That was where the problems started. Two men were there, and they noticed Frederic right away. He stopped trying to be stealthy then. He rushed the first man, knowing there was no way he could hold his own against two of them. He was lucky they hadn't shot him. It would have been easier and faster, at least for them.

He lowered his upper body and slammed into the first guy with his shoulder. He felt the air whoosh out of the man's lungs, but he didn't stop, slamming him into the closest wall. The impact jarred him into letting go and raising to his full height just in time to punch the guy in the face.

A man gripped his shoulder and twirled him around. Pain exploded in Frederic's cheekbone. He yelped and tried to move away, but the hand was still on his shoulder, squeezing to the point of pain.

Then it was gone. Frederic's eyes burned with suppressed tears as he watched Camden drag the man who'd punched him away and pushed him toward Griffin and Reece. Frederic was only slightly surprised to see his best friend there.

Camden turned toward Frederic. "Are you okay?"

Frederic rubbed his cheek and winced. "I've been better."

"You need something?"

"Just to go to Sam."

"Wait. Did you recognize any of these guys as the one who killed Sam's parents? You saw him earlier today."

Frederic didn't want to waste time, but Sam had said he'd noticed three motorcycles, so hopefully, the bad guys were all there.

They dragged all three of the men in the living room and turned on the lights. Frederic's stomach dropped. "Shit. He's not here."

Camden frowned. "Are you sure?"

"Yes." Frederic moved closer, but he was sure of it. "He had long hair." And all three of these guys had short hair. Frederic supposed the guy could have cut his, but he would have recognized him. He wasn't there.

Sam.

Frederic ran out of the living room, ignoring Camden and Reece's calls. He climbed the stairs two at a time. He slipped on the rug on top of the stairs and slammed against the wall, but it wasn't enough to make him stop.

The bedroom door was open, and he knew what he'd find there.

It was empty. Sam was nowhere to be seen, and while Frederic wanted to believe he was just in the bathroom, he knew better. His wolf growled and snarled, wanting release to go after the man who had taken their mate.

Frederic let him.

His jeans exploded around him as he shifted. Fur sprouted from his skin, and he turned to the door. He was going to go after that asshole and tear him apart for touching Sam.

Camden blocked the bedroom door. Frederic growled at him, but he didn't move, crossing his arms over his chest and glaring at him instead. "Really, Frederic?" he asked.

Frederic barked. Camden didn't move.

"I'll let you pass, but only if you allow me and Reece to come with you and if you start thinking. I know you want to kill that guy, but you can't. We need him to find out where Sam's brother is. You know Sam would never forgive you if you took that chance away from him."

Frederic forced himself to think. Camden was right. The thing Sam wanted the most in the world was to find his brother, and Frederic couldn't take that possibility away from him. He needed to think, even though it was hard. He could smell Sam. His scent was strong on the bed, mixed with Frederic's, but there was also a trail that led out of the bedroom, and there was another scent attached to it, so much that Frederic knew they'd been touching. The man who'd taken his mate had been overpowering him, holding him close to his body to make sure he didn't do something stupid like trying to escape.

Frederic was going to kill him.

After he got the information they needed out of him, of course.

He briefly closed his eyes and nodded. Camden relaxed and stripped, taking much too long for Frederic's tastes. Frederic barked at him again and walked around him. He might as well get a head start. Camden could catch up once he was done being the slowest man in the world.

He ran out of the house, following Sam's trail. He was going to find him this time. He wouldn't stop until he did.

They weren't far. From what Frederic could hear once he got close enough, Sam wasn't going quietly. He was complaining that the man still hadn't told him where his brother was, and he was dragging his feet.

"Just tell me if he'll be present when we get there," Sam said.

"Shut up."

"You said he would. You lied."

"And you were stupid enough to believe me. I sold your brother three years ago, boy."

That was the wrong thing to say, but then this guy didn't know Sam. Frederic was still too far to intervene, but he heard the sound of flesh pounding against flesh, a grunt and a yelp, Sam swearing. Then there was the sound of a slap and Sam's voice was pained. The smell of blood reached Frederic's nose, and he ran faster.

He saw Sam first, sitting on the ground, his back leaning against a tree. He was holding his face and looking at the man hovering over him with a hatred Frederic wouldn't have thought he was capable of feeling. Frederic focused on the other man. He couldn't kill him, but he could give him a few nips. Camden hadn't said anything about not scaring him, right?

Sam saw the wolf from the corner of his eye and jerked back. He knew it had to be a pack member and that they'd be careful not to hurt him, but he couldn't risk it, not when they might get him by accident while fighting the man who'd killed his parents.

The wolf latched onto the man's wrist, and the man screamed. He shook his arm in an attempt to get the wolf off, but it didn't work, and Sam was pretty sure that the crunching sound he heard was the bones in the man's wrist.

Then he realized *Frederic* was the wolf munching away on the man.

He should have seen it sooner, but it was dark, and he wasn't in an observant state of mind right now. "Don't kill him!" he yelled. He didn't dare get any closer, though. Frederic looked pissed, and Sam wondered if he might bite the man's hand off. It wouldn't kill him, so he'd still be able to answer questions. Or would the blood loss be debilitating?

Damn it. Sam hated having to go to the man's rescue, but

what else was he supposed to do? He couldn't let the man die, not if he wanted to find Toby.

Another two wolves barged in from between the trees. Sam pressed his back against a tree and watched them, unsure who they were. He was familiar with Frederic's wolf form by now, but while he'd seen several other pack members going around as wolves, he didn't exactly wait for them to shift back to human usually. It just wasn't okay to stare after a shift, except of course with your mate—and Sam had taken advantage of that plenty of times.

One of the wolves raised his head and howled. The sound seemed to resonate in Sam's body, in his bones, and he shivered. The other wolf came closer to him and shifted. He averted his eyes and looked up at Reece's face, but Reece didn't seem to care. He leaned closer to Sam and raised a hand as if to touch him. "Are you okay?"

Sam nodded. "I'm fine." The man who'd killed his parents hadn't hurt him. He hadn't had to, and Sam had heard him mutter about damaging the goods. He could only imagine what that meant, and he hoped it referred to a unicorn's healing power being focused on the unicorn itself rather than on others when it was hurt.

The man screamed louder, jarring Sam. His eyes widened when he saw that Frederic had bitten the man's ankle now. He could see the man's hand was limp, so he'd probably been right about the bones in his wrist being broken, and it looked like Frederic was doing the same to the man's ankle now.

The wolf growled at Frederic, but Frederic didn't seem to care. Sam looked at Reece, wondering what they were supposed to do. He wanted to let Frederic hurt the man who'd hurt him so much, but he wasn't sure they could risk it, not when Toby's life might be at stake.

"Come on. Let's stop him before he does too much damage," Reece said.

Sam wasn't eager to place himself between Frederic's fangs and the man who'd ruined his life, but he knew Frederic would regret it if he killed the man, and Sam hated the thought of Frederic being unhappy, especially for something like this.

The other wolf—Sam still didn't know who it was—was snipping at Frederic's haunches, but Frederic didn't seem to notice. Sam cautiously moved closer, but he let Reece take the lead. He'd been dealing with wolves all his life. He *was* a wolf. He'd know what to do.

"Freddy?" Reece said, his voice steady and calm.

Frederic growled without letting go of the man's ankle. The man wasn't screaming anymore. He was whimpering now, so Sam wasn't worried about him. If he could whimper, it meant he was still alive, and that was all that mattered.

"Come on, Freddy," Reece coaxed. "Sam's here, and he wants to find his brother. Remember? We need this guy to find Tobias. That means you have to stop hurting him so we can get answers out of him. It's the only way to find Tobias."

Frederic stopped growling. He looked at Sam, and Sam smiled in what he hoped was a reassuring smile. "Frederic? I need a hug after what happened. Do you think you can let go and shift? I'd rather have you human than furry."

That did it. Frederic dropped the man's ankle. He licked his chops, and Sam hoped he wasn't going to throw up. He hated seeing Frederic dirty with blood, not because of what he'd done but of what he'd been *pushed* to do. He'd been protecting Sam. That was the only reason he'd been violent.

Reece cleared his throat. "You should probably shift and clean up."

This time, Frederic obeyed. He shifted and rubbed his hands over his mouth. It really only transferred the blood, but it was better. And when he took Sam into his arms, Sam forgot all about blood and gore. He wasn't about to make out with his mate, but he could cuddle up to him while Reece and Camden grabbed the man from the ground and dragged him against a tree.

"I'm going to lose my foot," the man whined.

Sam didn't care, but he was doing this for Toby. He took a deep breath and turned toward the man. He tried to ignore the blood as he faced him. "Tell me where my brother is."

"My foot. I need my foot."

Sam wanted to kick him until he actually lost his damn foot. "I'll heal you if you tell me where Toby is."

Reece swore while Frederic's hold on Sam tightened. He didn't say anything, though, and Sam was glad.

The man on the ground looked up at him. "You will?"

"Yes. Tell me where Toby is."

It was surprisingly easy to get answers out of the man once Sam had promised to heal him.

"He's in the city. I sold him to a gang."

Sam's stomach dropped. "A gang?" What had they done to Toby?

"Yeah. They use him to heal their members after they fight and whatnot."

"That's all they did to him?"

"I don't know. I haven't seen him since I sold him. I heard of him, and he's only ever associated with healing in conversations, but I don't know."

"The address. Now."

"I don't know where they keep him."

Sam stepped closer to the man and kicked his broken ankle. The man screamed, and Sam wasn't even sorry. He'd do much worse if he had to. He'd do *anything* to get Toby back.

"All right, all right. I can tell you where the gang stays."

Sam had no idea where that place was when the man finally told him and the others, but that didn't matter. It was the next step in finding Toby.

"You told us everything you know?" he asked.

The man nodded. "Yes. I swear. I haven't seen your brother since the day I sold him."

Sam turned around and headed home, Frederic right behind him.

"Hey! You said you were going to heal me!"

Sam ignored the asshole on the ground. He didn't care if the man died from blood loss, if he lost his foot, or if he never walked again. He could rot in Hell, and Sam wouldn't care one bit. He didn't look back—all his thoughts were focused on going home. He knew what was waiting for him over the rest of the night—Camden would come around, they'd talk about what they'd found out tonight, and the research Camden was going to do to find Tobias. Sam's first instinct was to find a way to go to the city and get to his brother, but he had no idea where to start. He was at the mercy of the pack, of Camden, and he didn't like it, but he wasn't stupid enough not to realize this was the best way to do things. Going on his own would only get him and probably Toby killed, and Sam couldn't allow that to happen. Toby had suffered enough, but he'd been away for three years. One more night wouldn't change anything.

Of course, Sam had to believe he'd only been forced to heal. He hoped that was true.

He prayed it was.

Frederic had to stop and shift because he wasn't used to going around barefoot through the forest, but he quickly caught up to Sam. Sam was too focused on his thoughts to even realize Frederic had lost him for a moment, but Frederic wasn't offended. Sam had just been kidnapped and found, had to watch Frederic munch on the guy who'd killed his parents and had taken his brother, and had forced the guy to tell him where Tobias was.

It hadn't been an easy night for him.

It hadn't been for anyone, and it wasn't over yet.

They got home, and Sam hesitated. He turned slightly toward Sage's house. It was dark and silent, just like the rest of the houses, and Frederic wasn't ready to let Sam go. Besides, Camden would be on his way to talk to them as soon as he made sure the bleeding man was taken care of. They might as well stay in Frederic's house for now.

He shifted and put a hand on the small of Sam's back. "Come on. I need a shower and clothes, and you should probably sit down."

Sam chuckled. "I'm not sure I'll be able to get back up if I do. I can't remember ever feeling so tired."

"It's the adrenaline. You can rest on the couch while I shower. I'm sure Camden will be done by the time I'm finished."

Frederic made sure Sam was comfortable, wrapping his shoulders in a blanket without caring that he was still naked. He didn't miss the glances Sam gave his body, but neither of them was in the mood for anything related to sex.

Frederic hated leaving Sam on his own in a moment like this, but he really needed to shower. His hands and arms were dirty with blood, as well as his mouth, of course. He was pretty sure he had bits of the man he'd bitten caught between his teeth, and he couldn't wait to brush them—and use a lot of mouthwash. Maybe half the bottle.

He did quick work of cleaning up and refreshing his breath. Sam was still there when he went downstairs, curled up on the couch. Frederic sat next to him and opened his arms, and Sam crawled into them, settling onto Frederic's lap, his head against Frederic's chest.

Frederic stroked his hand up and down Sam's back. "Are you really okay?" he asked.

Sam nodded. His cheek rubbed against Frederic's t-shirt. "I'm tired, and I could have done without having to run around the woods barefoot, but I'm fine."

"Are you hurt? Because I can go grab a first aid kit." Frederic really should have thought about that sooner.

"I had some scratches, but I healed. Unicorn sifter, remember?"

Frederic nuzzled Sam's hair. "Right. I forget sometimes."

"How can you forget that? It's the most important part of me."

"Nope. You're just Sam to me. Not a unicorn shifter. I don't care about that, even though I'm glad you healed yourself."

Sam tilted his face toward Frederic, and Frederic kissed his forehead. "You really see me that way?"

"Yes. I don't see a healer when I look at you. That's a small part of you."

"What do you see, then?"

"You. A man who enjoys reading but doesn't like to show it because he thinks it's a waste of time he could spend studying instead. A man who likes chocolate and can eat the entire bar if I don't hide it from him even if it makes him sick. A man who likes watching superhero movies and romantic comedies but hates drama and cries when animals die even though he knows it's not reality. I see my future when I look at you, Sam. That's all."

Sam blinked. "All? You had plenty to say."

There was a quick knock on the front door, so Frederic didn't answer. Camden walked in without asking if he could, and Frederic grinned at him. "I see you have no problem just walking in."

"Just like you shouldn't at my house, but I've already

been over that, and you don't listen to me, so let's skip right ahead to what's happening, okay?"

Frederic waved toward the armchair. "Sit down."

"First things first. Sam, are you okay?"

Frederic snorted. "I'm hurt. Do I mean so little to you?"

Sam chuckled, and Frederic felt ten feet tall because of that. He'd made Sam laugh even now that he was no doubt worried sick about his brother and wanting to go get him. He might have gone if he knew how to drive, actually. Frederic wouldn't have been surprised.

Camden rolled his eyes, but his smile was soft and understanding. "I can see you're okay. Besides, you weren't the one in need of a healer after that little scene in the forest."

Frederic shrugged. "I regret nothing."

"I sure hope you don't. That guy's an asshole. He deserves everything he got. I was tempted not to ask Naila to help him, but he might be useful. If we can take out the entire ring of hunters and traffickers, it'll be worth it."

"As long as I don't have to work on him with Naila, I agree," Sam said.

"You don't. I asked Reece to explain what was happening to her. She'll take care of him."

Sam straightened on Frederic's lap. "Did he say anything else about Toby?"

"Nah. He mostly whined and cried, which is understandable considering his wrist and ankle look like hamburger meat."

"So we don't know where to find the gang that bought my brother."

Camden leaned back and rubbed his face. "Not exactly. I've heard of them, and I know some of the shifters in the city have been having problems with them, but I haven't asked for details. It's none of my business, or it wasn't until now anyway. But I know people we can contact to find out where they are. It's just going to take a few hours to organize everything. Even once we know where the gang is. I'm going to try to find out if your brother is still with them. Once we know if he is, we can decide how to enter."

"And if he's not? I have a hard time believing a gang kept him safe for three years," Frederic said. He didn't like to think about the alternatives, but someone had to.

"They still have him," Sam said. He sounded confident, as if he knew something Frederic and Camden didn't.

"How do you know?" Frederic made sure his voice was steady. He wanted to believe Sam, but there was no way he could be sure about this.

"Toby is a healer, like me. He's too valuable to give away or even to resell, not unless the gang made a huge profit from it. I *can* see that happening, but that man said they'd bought him to heal gang members, and from the little I know about gangs, I'm pretty sure they need him weekly, if not more often. He'd be more valuable than any amount of money. Trust me on that."

"I think he's right," Camden agreed. "I'm going to do my best to find out if Tobias is with the gang, but we can probably plan this with that in mind."

"I want to come," Sam said.

Frederic wasn't surprised, and from Camden's expression, neither was he. "Are you sure it's a good idea?" Frederic asked. He wouldn't tell Sam he couldn't go, but he wanted to be sure Sam had thought about it beyond what he was feeling. It was natural that he wanted to be one of those who'd free his brother, but could he really do it without endangering himself, Tobias, and the people who'd help them?

"I'll stay back and wait for whoever is in charge to tell me to come in, but I want to be there. Toby's been with strangers long enough. He'll be terrified, and I want him to know I'm there for him. I'll obey whatever orders you want me to obey, I'll do whatever you want me to do, but please, don't ask me to stay here while you go."

Camden rubbed the back of his head. "All right. You can come, as long as like, you said, you obey orders." He sighed. "I've already called a few people, so I hope to have all the info we need to plan this by morning."

"It's already morning," Frederic pointed out. It was going on five AM.

Camden waved. "We all need to go to bed, though, you two included. I know it's not going to be easy to sleep, but things would go more smoothly and safely if we're all as rested as we can be. Sleep, eat, and meet me at my house at twelve. We'll talk again then."

Chapter Seven

Sam bit his lower lip and looked at the building in front of him. "Are you *sure* this is where the gang lives?"

Camden grinned. "Yep. I double checked."

It wasn't what Sam had expected. He'd thought they'd find Toby in a dirty cold warehouse or something like that, not in a villa that looked like it wouldn't be out of place on a beach. "But it's so . . . ."

"Normal?"

"Not exactly." Sam was sure plenty of people lived in places like this, but he preferred the smaller, homier homes in pack territory. This house was much bigger and luxurious, at least from the inside. He could imagine those actors he watched on TV living there, not gang members.

Frederic's arm tightened around Sam's waist, and he pulled Sam closer. He kissed Sam's temple. "I know you want to go in."

"Of course I do. But I promised." At least Frederic was staying with him. He wouldn't have to worry that his mate might be hurt. He was already worrying enough about Toby.

God, Sam couldn't believe his brother was there, so close that he'd see him in the next half hour. He swallowed and prayed that was true, that Camden was right and that this was the place where the gang lived. He wasn't sure what he'd do if they didn't find Toby today.

"I'll let you know as soon as it's safe to come in," Camden said.

He left them behind. Sam wasn't sure where he'd found the people helping them, and he didn't care much. He was glad they looked like they knew what they were doing, though. He didn't want anyone to get hurt, not his brother, and not any of the pack members who'd volunteered to come. Sam hadn't thought so many of them would, yet there they were—Reece, Griffin—Camden's beta—Jarvis, and another two men Sam didn't think he'd ever talked to. Even Sage had wanted to come, but Camden had dissuaded him. Sam was glad for that. He wasn't a fighter, and neither was Sage. He would never forgive himself if he lost someone he considered his best friend to this, even if they did manage to get Toby back.

Sam clutched Frederic's hand as they both watched Camden and the others sneak into the house. Naila was there, too, just in case Toby or anyone else needed her. Sam would have offered his services as a healer, but Toby probably had more experience than he did in that, and this would be the worst moment to fuck things up.

"How long do you think it's going to take?" he asked after what felt like an hour but was probably more like five minutes.

"I don't know. They're going to have to go through every room. Camden's objective is to find Tobias, but the others want to take down the gang. This is a prime opportunity for them to do it. They bought a unicorn shifter. Of course, if they deal in drugs and other stuff, buying your brother is the least of their problems, but still."

Sam knew all that, but his mind couldn't seem to be able to focus on anything but Toby. Was he really in that house? Was he okay? What had happened to him during the past three years? Sam did and didn't want to know at the same time. He wanted to be there for Toby and know what to do to help him, but the thought of his sweet little brother going through whatever horror he'd gone through was terrifying for Sam. He couldn't imagine what it had been like for Toby.

Someone in the house screamed. Sam squeezed Frederic's hand even harder and fought the urge to run and check whether it had been Toby or one of the other people he cared about.

"They'll be okay," Frederic said. Sam was glad for his attempt to reassure him, but it wasn't working. Still, it gave him something else to focus on, which was a good thing once the gunshots started.

Sam felt like he held his breath through it all. He didn't know how much time had passed when the front door slammed open so hard it probably left indents in the wall. Two people ran out, quickly followed by another two. Sam could still hear shots, so he knew this wasn't over. He leaned forward, trying to see who those people running away were. Were some gang members trying to escape? He wouldn't be surprised, but it didn't look like it, because instead of running along the sidewalk and trying to leave, they came right toward him and Frederic.

Sam's heart raced. "Is that him?" he asked even though Frederic wouldn't know. Sam had refused to go back to his parents' home for now, so he didn't even have a picture. It was too soon for him, but he'd go back one day, and he hoped Toby would be with him then. That meant Frederic had no idea what Toby looked like, though, so he couldn't answer Sam's question.

He didn't need to.

Camden was one of the men in the front, and he was half carrying the other man. He didn't seem to be having a hard time with it because the other man was small, much smaller than him—about Sam's height, and just as thin. Sam couldn't see his face, though, because the man was leaning against Camden's chest, with Camden's arm around his shoulders holding him close.

Then Camden and the man stepped onto the sidewalk. Sam recognized Reece and Jarvis behind them, but he barely glanced at them. He stepped forward, and Frederic moved with him, but he let go of him, so Sam was free to rush forward as soon as the light of the street lamp shone on Toby's face.

Sam noticed Camden steel himself just before he slammed into him, his arms wrapping around his brother without a conscious decision from him. Toby made a strangled sound and tried to push away for just a second. Then he sucked in a breath and grabbed Sam, holding onto him as hard as Sam as doing with him.

"Sam!" he yelled.

Sam felt Camden try to extricate himself from the group hug, then give up. He gently pushed them toward Frederic instead. "Come on, guys. Let's get off the sidewalk. I'm sure Tobias could use a moment to rest."

Sam didn't want to let go, but he knew Camden was right. He stepped back, grabbing one of Toby's hands because he wasn't ready to let go just yet, and let Camden guide Toby toward the truck they'd arrived in. Naila and Sam had made sure there would be everything Toby might need in it—clean clothes, blankets, water, snacks, medical supplies, even shoes. But Toby was dressed in jeans and an old t-shirt, so they wouldn't need all of it. He didn't look like he'd been wounded, although he might have already healed, and he appeared, well, better than what Sam had expected. He was thin, but not too much, his hair was short and cared for, and he was beaming.

Sam swallowed. He wasn't sure where to start, what to tell Toby. He'd thought about this moment for years, and now that he was living it, he couldn't speak. He could only hold onto Toby.

Camden helped Toby sit in the backseat. Sam had to let go, but he rushed around the truck and climbed in next to his brother. They both reached for each other at the same time, and Sam buried his nose against Toby's neck, breathing him in. "God, I didn't think I'd ever see you again," he murmured.

Toby's hands clenched in Sam's shirt. "Same. I thought I'd have to spend the rest of my life in this place. I can't believe you're here. How did you find me? How did you escape when the men came to take us? Where have you been all this time?"

Shit. Was Toby aware their parents were dead? He hadn't asked about them, so Sam suspected he was, but he needed to be sure. "Mom told me to run. I hid in the forest."

"Please tell me you had help to deal with them after."

Sam choked on tears. "I've been living in the forest since then."

Toby gently pushed him away. He was the youngest, but he reached up and dried the tears from Sam's cheeks. "Sammy. God, I hate that you had to go through this on your own." He smiled. "But you're not alone anymore, are you?"

Sam shook his head. "I'm not. I met my mate."

Toby's smile widened. "Yeah? And he's a member of that pack who lived near us?"

"He is."

"That's great. So is my mate."

Sam blinked. "Your mate?" What was Toby talking about?

Toby's gaze slid to the front of the truck. "Yes. He said his name is Camden."

YOU MAY ALSO ENJOY THE FOLLOWING FROM EXTASY BOOKS INC:

Brandon
Catherine Lievens

Excerpt

Maddox crouched in front of the cage and silently opened it. The Beagle inside looked at him with his big eyes—eyes Maddox couldn't say no to. "Come on, Colonel Bau. Let's get you out of here."

He wiggled his fingers, and the dog moved toward him. They were already friends since Maddox had been taking care of him since he'd arrived at the shelter. He trusted Maddox, and Maddox laughed when he licked his face. "Good boy. Come on. I'm taking you home." And so what if that meant Asher was right and that Maddox had more animal friends than human ones? Colonel Bau needed him, and he needed the unconditional love his furry friends gave him. At least they would never kick him out or abandon him. Besides, he only had two dogs. He could take in a third, especially when he was as cute as Colonel Bau was.

Maddox had already filled in and signed all the forms for the adoption, so he hooked the leash onto Colonel Bau's collar and led him to the exit. He'd waited until everyone else was gone so Asher wouldn't bug him about taking in another dog, so he made a quick exit, hauling Colonel Bau into his truck and driving toward home. He relaxed as he did so, happy to be going home, and to have another dog. He loved animals, and he'd seen enough of Colonel Bau to know he loved him back. The poor dog didn't deserve to spend the rest of his life in the shelter, and since he was an older dog, people weren't fighting to adopt him.

Well, that wasn't a problem now. Maddox had adopted him, and when he took in an animal, it was for life. Colonel Bau was set.

The dog was slightly wary when Maddox led him into his new home, probably a mix of being in a new place and the smells and sounds of the other animals living there. Maddox left the Beagle in his living room and went to free his other two dogs—Madame Mimsy and Princess Pawpington—from their crates. They ran around his ankles as Queen Elizabeth watched them from her spot on the kitchen counter. She was a fluffy, haughty cat, and she didn't like being cuddled, although she sometimes made an exception for Maddox.

"All right, all right. Give me the time to take everything out, and I'll feed you, loves," Maddox told the animals as he moved around the kitchen.

That seemed to be the magic word. Colonel Bau appeared at the kitchen door, followed by Lord Nibbles and King McFluff, two of Maddox's cats. The last one, Prince Whiskerton, was always late, so Maddox wasn't worried that he wasn't here yet.

He busied himself with the food, dishing it and putting down all the bowls in his usual order—first the cats because they wouldn't listen to him when he told them to stay, then the dogs, who usually obeyed him. Colonel Bau got his own bowl—Maddox always had a few of those around, just in case.

Once that was done, he fed his parrot, Fitz, then brought

carrots and lettuce out to his two rabbits, Bugs and Bunny. Once that was done, it was time for Maddox to take care of himself. He stuck some leftovers in the microwave and headed for the bathroom as they heated, but he stopped when he heard the sound of tires on the gravel outside his house. He didn't often get visitors, and even when he did, it wasn't late at night. Of course, it was late only for him since his friends didn't think anything of going out at ten PM, but he had to work tomorrow, and he still had to shower and eat. It was already eight-thirty PM, so he wouldn't have a lot of time to relax and read, especially not with Colonel Bau being new.

Maddox could hear voices and footsteps. He sighed when he recognized one of the voices as Asher's and walked to the front door before he could knock. He opened it, and sure enough, Asher's fist was raised. He almost knocked on Maddox's nose, chuckling when he noticed the open door. "Oops. Hey, Maddox."

Asher wasn't alone. Terry was with him—of course he was, when did those two ever do something without the other—as well as Gabriel and Alice. Maddox was friends with all of them, but that didn't mean he was happy to see them. He liked his friends in small doses, which meant not all together. "This looks like an intervention." He wouldn't be surprised if it were, not after the conversation he'd had with Asher.

Asher grimaced. "It kind of is? I mean, it's not an intervention per se, but everyone was worried about you, so we decided to come around and see if we could drag you out or something."

Alice pushed past Maddox, ignoring his scowl. "We're taking you to the club to dance. I'm picking your clothes. Do you have anything that's not covered in animal hair?"

"I didn't invite you to come in," he yelled after her, but she ignored him.

He wasn't surprised. He turned his attention back to Asher and gave him his best glare. "I don't want to go dancing. I hate dancing and clubs."

"Maybe, but it will do you good to come. You spend too much time with your cats." He cocked his head and looked at something behind Maddox. "And your dogs. All three of them."

Maddox didn't blush. Nope. "What?"

"I see Colonel Bau has a new home."

"He was lonely at the shelter."

"Well, he sure won't be here. I think Prince Whiskerton likes him."

Terry made a strangled sound. Maddox glared at him, too, even though he was probably the only one who couldn't have cared less if Maddox went dancing with their little group. He was Asher's mate, but that didn't mean he and Maddox were friends. "What?" Maddox snapped.

Terry shook his head. "Nothing. I mean . . . Prince Whiskerton?"

"I don't think the way I name my pets is any of your business."

Asher grinned and turned to look at his mate. "Wait until you meet Princess Pawpington and Lord Nibbles."

That did it. Terry giggled, then pressed his lips together, but Maddox could see he was about to explode. He rolled his eyes and stepped aside to let the buggers in. He scowled at Gabriel, too, even though the poor guy hadn't said anything and was probably there because Alice had dragged him along. They were kindred spirits, happier with staying home than going out but going anyway to make their friends happy.

Pity they weren't all of the furry kind because Maddox had no problem dealing with those.

He left the three in his living room fawning over his pets and went to his bedroom. He grimaced when he saw the result of Alice's nosiness. Half of his wardrobe was on the bed, the other half precariously hanging from Alice's arm as she examined every single piece of clothing before dumping it with the rest.

She looked up when Maddox came in. "Mad, do you really not have anything nice looking?"

Maddox looked down at himself. He was the first to admit his clothes weren't great, but he was comfortable, and that was what mattered to him. "My pets don't care how I look."

"And you clearly don't, either." She held up a pair of black jeans Maddox couldn't remember buying. "Okay, let's go with this, but don't let any of your cats and whatnot come close enough to get fur on it."

"Alice—"

"Nope. I'm not taking no for an answer. You're going to become a hermit if someone doesn't drag you out of here."

"I go to work every day."

"Yeah, and you work with animals. Not people. That doesn't count."

"I buy groceries."

She narrowed her eyes. "Look, we can do this my way, which is definitely the easiest way, or the harder way."

Maddox wasn't sure he wanted to know what that implied. He sighed heavily and took the jeans from her hands. "Fine."

She beamed. "Great! We're going to have fun, you'll see."

Maddox had a hard time believing that, but he didn't say it out loud. He didn't want to make Alice angry or sad. As long as she didn't try to get him to go dancing again in the next two or three months, he supposed he could do this.

About the Author

Catherine lives in Italy, country of good food and hot men. She used to write fantasy as a child, but it was reading her first gay erotic romance novel that made her realize that that was what she really wanted to write.

After graduating from college in English language and translation, she divides her day between writing, reading, taking care of her son and reading some more.

You can find her on Facebook and Twitter or on her website: authorcatherinelievens.wordpress.com

Email: lievens.catherine@gmail.com

Newsletter: http://eepurl.com/c-uvKn

www.ingramcontent.com/pod-product-compliance
Lightning Source LLC
Chambersburg PA
CBHW060633130626
46555CB00002B/776